I0714232

DEREK HEATH

RED SKY
ALL
NIGHT

POPE LICK PRESS

2024

"When it is evening, ye say, fair weather: for the heaven is red. And in the morning, foul weather today for the heaven is red and lowering."

Matthew 16:2-3

"Red sky at night, shepherd's delight.
Red sky in the morning, shepherds take warning..."

Old adage, adapted to rhyme from
the Bible passage above

"The Goat Sucker Heads North: A long-clawed, lizard-like monster known as the Chupacabra (Spanish for Goat Sucker) has spawned a fad and sent cash registers ringing along the border with Mexico."

From the *Baltimore Times*
August 30th 1996

"Into the yard it creeps, while you are asleep, and sucks your goat: The chupacabra may or may not exist, but it's selling an awful lot of T-shirts."

From the *Corpus Christi Caller Times*
April 28th 1996

<u>Chapter One</u>
MUTILATED

Nyth Farm, Herefordshire
1996

In the brooding shadow of the Black Mountains to the west, blood seeped through the grass of a ragged field and the thick, coppery scent of death rolled on the mist.

The late hours of the day passed slowly and without witness. The roads that diverged from Nyth Farm and canted through the fields toward both Peterchurch and Hay-on-Wye were winding, narrow lanes of tarmac that slid and crawled down the hills all round; this time of day, the roads were empty. Even the two or three cars that passed by would not have seen the carnage in the soiled field, for the headlights were trained forward and the drivers too focused on the path ahead; no, the bodies would not be discovered until the early hours of the morning.

The first sign of life was a light in the farmhouse, barely visible from the road, and minutes later a second light in the low, wooden-walled barn at the edge of the field. A rooster called from downwind; the sound was lost.

The farmhouse was a smudge of red and brown a mile or so from the road, and though a crumbling dirt track – walled on either side by stacks of slim flintstones – led to the driveway and feed store, the farm's owner barely drove save to fetch groceries once a week and to visit Morgana and the kids in The Bage every second Tuesday. Farmer Lewis owned the farmhouse, the silo, the barn and a hundred and ten acres of land, and he rarely stepped outside of the boundary of those ten acres save to walk to the common and back every few nights. Dr Thomas had told him to keep his joints supple as he could in his advancing age. At forty-nine, Lewis had scoffed; at fifty-four, he saw the appeal.

The morning light was soft and grey and a low blanket of fog seemed to roll down from the mountains and slide through the crooked husks of trees on the common before spilling onto the road and surrounding the farm. Had the air been clear, he would have seen all the blood from his bedroom window. As it was, the mist crept through the fields and almost turned pinkish as particles of spilled meat crested on it. The sheep in the next-door field – thirty of Lewis's hundred-and-ten acres – bleated continually, stress pitching and keening on the wind. Both this sound and the stink of blood carried downwind, and like the calling of the rooster, both were lost.

A little after five-thirty, Farmer Lewis crossed the fields with a sealed, metal pail of feed in each hand. He visited the sheep first and set one bucket in the north corner of their field. Beside a crumbling brick wall, the top of which had been strung up with barbed wire, he popped the lid open and waited for them to come.

They did not.

He could hear them squawking now, the strangled mewls of the lambs batted away by the deep, mournful wails of their mothers, but usually when they heard the *tok* of the metal lid bending open they swarmed upon him and he could leave them to feed from it while he moved to the south corner and opened the second pail. After a few minutes or so they would grow bored and disperse again across the field; the food would last for two or three days.

This morning, he was left standing by the pail with the mist tugging and clawing at his calves.

Silently, Lewis left the bucket and tramped across the field, careful not to step in any spoors. His wellingtons were heavy and his feet squelched in the damp earth as he walked. It was lambing season, and he feared the worst: perhaps one of the ewes had miscarried, and he'd find the poor creature in a pool of her own slick, purple fluid, the others standing sombrely around her.

After he'd set the second pail down – still he was without company, though he'd been as loud about his movements as he thought possible – Gwynne Lewis followed the sounds of bleating and ventured through the mist.

Ahead of him, the road and the fields and commons were completely obscured by that thick, torn blanket of white and grey, though the dark shapes of the Black Mountains rose like peaks of the fog itself had been drawn up into the sky. Long slopes of shadow dipped and swung and crashed together.

He smelled blood.

Lewis quickened his pace, eyes scouring the mist for signs of life. When he had nearly reached the road, shapes began to jut out of the swampy, ever-thickening groundcover, and in moments those shapes had become the tipping heads of sheep. Lambs skittered uneasily about his feet as he joined the throng at the fence, trying to follow their gaze into the next field but unable to see much further than ten feet in front of him. The awful wailing sound was deafening, and he tried to hush them, but their distress was palpable and he could taste fear on the soft, slow breeze. He was certain that they could not see anything either, though they seemed transfixed on something in the other field.

Perhaps it was not one of the sheep who had miscarried after all, he thought. He stood among them for a minute, his shins and knees bumped by the shuffling, despairing things as they milled about and knotted together, becoming deformed, fused-together creatures in the mist. The abominable shapes fussed around him, nudging him toward the fence, urging him to take a look for himself.

Farmer Lewis was about to climb the fence into the goats' field when he heard a scream.

It came from the roadside.

'Hello?' Lewis called, turning toward the sound and raising a hand to his brow as though to shield his eyes – either from the glowing white of the mist or the cascading, blinding black of the mountains beyond – but there was no sign of anybody at the road save for the suffocating aura of fear on the fog, which had inched a notch tighter. 'Hello, who's—'

'Gwynne?' someone called from the road. The

voice was that of a young man, with a soft, pleasant Welsh accent. It was about three pitches higher than it should have been, and the echoes of the scream lingered on it still. 'Gwynne, is that you? You need to see this!'

Lewis stumbled through the barricade of shuffling creatures around him, heading for the fence. Though he could not see the road, the sloping vision of the mountains in the distance guided him in the right direction. 'Out of the way,' he mumbled, gently pushing a distressed ewe away from him.

Reaching the fence, he tipped a discarded hunk of log onto its end and used it to step up and over. He barely noticed the pain as a point of barbed wire pricked the soft flesh of his hand between thumb and forefinger. Sticky warmth spread across his palm and he stepped into the road.

A shadow moved toward him, lurching through the fog.

'Adrian, is that you?' Lewis called. Black clods of thick, damp earth splashed the tarmac in his wake. The shadow came forward from the mist, red-faced and wide-eyed. Fearful. 'Christ, what is it, man? What's going on? The sheep are—'

'Forget the sheep, Gwynne,' Adrian said, shaking his head and gesturing behind him. He was a farmer's boy, but not a farmer: short, black hair;

clean-shaven and smooth with city hands, clean hands. 'Come take a look…'

The goats, Lewis realised. The field all the sheep had been looking into, so despairing and mournful. Oh, not his goats…

He followed Adrian to the fence of the goat pen. Another twelve acres of clipped, rolling grassland, home to eight alpine goats that he'd bought off the young man's father three winters before. Between them they produced a good fifteen gallons of milk per day; during lambing season, they were Lewis's livelihood.

He could smell the blood now, thick and strong and gluey.

When he reached the fence, he realised he'd been walking through it.

It spilled beneath the crooked slats of the fence and onto the road, slarry rivers of red steaming in the cold. The steam mingled with mist and thin ribbons coiled around his ankles; his wellingtons were splashed crimson.

'No…' he moaned, gripping the fence with both hands and looking into the field. Behind him, Adrian laid a soft hand on the older man's shoulder and squeezed gently.

'I'm sorry, Gwynne,' the boy said. 'I'm so sorry.'

Gwynne Lewis shrugged off Adrian's hand and

shook his head. 'What could have done this?'

'A fox, maybe,' Adrian suggested weakly, 'or—'

'Weren't no fox,' Lewis said. 'Weren't nothing I know of.'

'I'm sorry,' Adrian said. 'Do you think it was the same thing that butchered poor Helen Jones' cat last week?'

Lewis said nothing. He swallowed bitterly, staring at the carnage as taut bands of mist rolled across the carcasses strewn over the grass.

'You know, I heard talk of a creature,' Adrian said. 'Last year. Puerto Rico. A vicious, demonic thing—'

'Weren't no demon,' Lewis said quietly.

'If it weren't a fox, though—'

'I said, it weren't no demon.'

'All right, well—'

'That's enough, Adrian,' Lewis said, his eyes never leaving the nearest cadaver. Bec was the oldest of the alpines he'd bought, and her milk was often sour and easy to spoil. Still, the well of her produce had not yet run dry, and he was always careful with her.

Always had been, anyway.

Farmer Lewis did not sob, but as he gazed down at the carcass of the old doe he found his breath hitched in his throat, his heartbeat fluttering and fast.

Whatever had done this to her – to all of them – had begun at her midsection, opening it wide and tipping her insides into the earth. It had not been interested in the slippery, translucent organs, or at least not interested enough to do more than nibble and puncture them. But apart from the blood that had congealed in the grass – perhaps that was spoiled, when it touched the ground – there was none left of her.

The thing had plunged its snout into her torso and drunk heavily from the deep, red well before cutting open her neck and sucking the rest of her life from her. She was spattered with sticky, solidifying ichor and her hooves were bloody where she'd kicked and fought. It hadn't cared. Deep, wet rends across her face were highlighted against the pallid, stiff coat of fur: deep welts of red among bony, pale curves of rigor mortis. She had been drained.

Lewis had named another of the goats Fand, for the spattering of white fur on her rump that looked like a bird with its wings spread; the brown had all faded so that now that mark was almost invisible. She lay just yards from Bec, and her wounds were less severe but the creature had drunk more fully from her; she was all bones, and the skin had almost sloughed off.

Two more of Lewis's goats lay in a mangled pile

by the water trough, their horns broken and splintered, bellies ruptured. One of Niamh's legs was broken and the bone had shot through and into Sadhbh's flank, but no blood spilled from the hole. The latter carcass had already been spent when the creature had flung the former into it.

'It drank their blood,' Lewis said, looking from one cadaver to the next with his own face drained of all colour. 'Good lord, it drank them dry.'

The goats lay sprawled in the grass, a mess of broken limbs and spilled insides, all of them thin and scrawny, bones pushing tightly against shrivelled skins. Glassy eyes rolled up in their heads, proud horns cracked and bent into the tops of their skulls. The creature hadn't just eaten and drunk from them, but had enjoyed it, too.

Played with them.

'Could only have been the Devil what done this,' Adrian said behind him.

'I think you misunderstand the Devil,' Lewis said. 'Besides, this weren't no Devil. Was an animal what done this.'

'A vampire, maybe.'

Lewis turned, cocking an eyebrow. His face, wrinkled and weathered from thirty-odd years of hard work, twisted into a frown. 'A vampire?'

'You don't believe there's things out there like

them?' Adrian said. 'There's demons and devils, for sure – Bigfoots and Yetis and everything in-between – why not vampires?'

'Vampire wouldn't have left the sheep alone,' Lewis said.

Adrian paused. 'Not one of them?'

'They're fine. Just pissing themselves.'

'It only went for the goats. The meat, perhaps—'

'Didn't take no meat,' Lewis said. 'Only the blood.'

'Then—'

'Then nothing,' Lewis said, turning back to the field. 'Call your father over, see if he wouldn't mind helping me clear this up. And keep quiet about it. You're a reasonable young lad, Ady, and even you're going off about Bigfoots – Bigfeet? – so lord knows what that lot'll say down in the village.'

'My father?' Adrian said. 'I could help—'

'You just fetch your father,' Lewis said. 'This is a job for people with country hands.'

Adrian looked at the old man for a long, hard second. 'You know, this thing they found in the Americas,' he said. 'They called it the goat-sucker. Drank from livestock like a vampire, except it was worse than that. Hungry, violent... rabid. An animal.'

'Your father,' Lewis said. 'Quick as you like.'

'They called it the *Chupacabra*.'

'I call it a whole lot of livestock dead and a young fella prattling about monsters. That's enough, Ady.'

Farmer Lewis stood there for a long time, staring out into the field, watching shadows slip through the mist and imagining that each one was slinking toward him on all fours, teeth bared and glowing white in the fog. Eventually his eyes lifted to the barn in the distance, to that low, red smudge – half of which was chewed up and spat out by the grey, smoky groundcover – and then they fell, again, to the broken carcasses in the field and he let himself weep.

When Adrian's father arrived at the roadside, the two spoke for a little while about foxes and wild dogs. Farmer Hyde speculated, just as his son had done, that whatever killed the goats might have been the same thing that killed poor Helen Jones' cat.

Then they began to clear the corpses, and that single, awful word echoed in Lewis's tired head. Over and over, bloodier and bloodier every time:

Chupacabra.

Chapter Two
RACHEL

Three miles from the Welsh-English Border
2021

The camper slowed to a rattling stop at the side of the road, pulling gently into a layby that crumbled at the edges and dipped and broke into ribbons of thick, clay soil. For a moment the Volkswagen T1 just sat there, bobbing slightly as the driver unbuckled her seatbelt and shuffled through the duffle bag perched on the passenger seat.

The layby was mottled with spots of white and grey; a dappled canopy lurched across it like a ceiling, branches reaching and clawing at the road from the tops of crooked trees beyond the verge. Nothing but rolling hillocks and fields for miles around.

The cab door opened suddenly, hinges groaning as it swung out over the wheel. The lower half of the T1 was painted a lurid yellow, spattered at the edges by baked on clumps of muck; the top was white, and the camper's roof gleamed in the pale sunlight. The driver stepped out, stretching her back and shoulders. Rachel Wheatley cricked her neck and winced, left leg almost dying on the spot. 'Christ,' she murmured to herself, looking up and down the road. She hadn't seen a single car for the last forty or fifty minutes of the drive – in fact, ever since leaving Ross-on-Wye, where she'd stopped to pick up some food and fill up the microbus, she hadn't seen another soul.

Rachel closed the cab door and moved to the back of the T1, bending down to check the rear tyre. Still full, despite the dreadful bang! she'd heard from the back of the van a little over twenty minutes ago. She had kept driving, so close to where she'd planned to spend the night that it didn't seem to matter if she hobbled the last leg; now, she was relieved there seemed to be no damage. Must have gone over something in the road, she thought.

Patting the rump of the camper, she moved around the back of the vehicle and explored the layby. Corduroy trousers chafed her stiff legs as she moved. She'd begun the drive from Inverness at a little after four in the morning and made good time; the sun was at its highest point in the sky and its mild, grey heat sunk wetly into her shoulders through the material of a thin, yellow blouse and brown jacket. Legs still stiff, she glanced up; nailed to a tree at the edge of the road, half-hidden in the shadow of the camper, was a ragged sign:

No parking overnight.

She sighed and looked around again. The road was still empty. She certainly hadn't seen any hotels around here, not in the last ten miles or so. And besides, what was the point of the T1 if she couldn't sleep in it?

Quickly, she moved back to the rear of the camper and popped open the storage trunk, stepping out of the way as the door swung down. Removing a small, plastic stepladder and a claw hammer, she glanced furtively about one last time before moving back to the tree and getting to work. Setting the stepladder at the base of the tree, she climbed awkwardly, tongue pressed to the back of her teeth as she raised the claw hammer and dug it behind the sign. Tipping the hammer back gently, she eased the nail loose and grabbed the sign as it came free. Hurrying back to the trunk, she tossed the hammer and stepladder – and the newly-vandalised sign – inside and locked it shut.

'Right,' Rachel said, wiping her palms on her corduroys. The thick fingers of a deep, Scottish accent clutched at every word. 'That's that taken care of.'

Disappearing inside the T1, she hastily prepared her bed for the night and switched her jacket and blouse for a thick, green jumper. Carefully, she unfolded a small wooden table and carried it outside, setting it down in the shadow of the camper. Returning inside momentarily, she brought out a crooked, plastic stool and a blue cooler, laying them both by the table. Making a third trip, she brought out a 1965 Webster Portable typewriter in both hands and put it carefully on the desk, sliding a sheet of paper into its mouth and perching herself on the stool.

'To work, then,' she told herself, before stopping to open the cool-box and open a bottle of Galahad. She drank steadily, putting the bottle down only when half the beer had been drained and returning to the typewriter. Finally, she said, 'To work, Rachel.'

For a full three minutes, she stared at the blank page, her fingers hovering over the keys. The typewriter was encased in hard, baby-blue plastic, the keys an ugly ivory like Scrabble tiles. It was unpleasant, but practical. And her neurons had been firing like cannons all the way here; she had driven in silence, contemplating new stories and scenes, thrilled at the speed and solidarity with which they came to her. And now she was here, ready to type, and…

Uninspired, Rachel looked with a sigh out into the landscape. Across the road, the rolling green of the fields dipped down into patches of yellow and brown, clipped blades of grass swaying in a light breeze. She fancied she could see Offa's Dyke from here: a long, crumbling wall of earth that separated England from Wales and that jutted unevenly from the ground all the way across her field of view.

She thought of ghosts, felt that she could see them crawling across the countryside; pale, slender shapes with slavering, broken jaws and fog shifting and rolling through their half-solid forms. She saw them clambering over the Dyke toward her, jerking and twisting as they writhed over the field. Dozens of them, ragged faces pulled about by the wind, eyes burning red…

Smiling, Rachel returned to the typewriter and got to work.

It was almost dark when Rachel finished her chapter with a crescendo of frantically-jabbed keys and leant back from the typewriter, knotting her fingers together and cracking the knuckles loudly.

She drank from the bottle on the desk and, when it was empty, laid it beside the others on the ground at her feet. She gently plucked the last page from the mouth of the typewriter and slid it into a pile that had accumulated on the edge of the desk. Thoughtfully, she read through the finished first chapter in the half-light. Satisfied, she stood up and prepared to take everything back into the camper.

As her eyes flitted up to the roadside, she saw a dark shape moving across the Dyke. It disappeared, as quick as it had come, and she blinked. Just her overactive imagination again, she thought, shrugging it off and turning to the desk to wrestle the unwieldy typewriter back inside.

And then she heard it. A scream, across the hills; not the scream of a person but the agonised, strangled wail of an animal caught in a trap. It echoed, rippling across the breeze for what felt like a lifetime, and then it died.

Rachel's blood ran cold. It had sounded like a horse caught in barbed wire, the unnatural sound ringing with fear and anguish and unearthly as though ragged claws had raked out the thing's windpipe and twisted its throat inside-out.

The wind ran cold and her heart fluttered with the echoing terror of that awful sound. She stood with her back to the camper and stared down at Offa's Dyke. Remembered the flitting shadow of the creature she'd seen just moments before.

'You're being thick,' she said quietly, turning back to the camper. As she stepped up through the door, she heard the sound of an engine and turned her head to see a little beaten-up Ford Orion, little more than a pale blue smudge winding its way up the slanted road toward her. 'You're being thick,' she said again, 'and I won't have it.'

With the memory of that scream ringing in her ears, she stepped into the T1 and closed the door behind her.

Ghost stories were easy. Ghost stories had been the thing to get Rachel Wheatley out of the slump of her mid-twenties: no longer was she working a dead-end job at an Inverness records and heritage office; no longer was she drinking before noon and wishing she was somewhere else all day, every day; she had started reading when she was a child, started writing when she was a teen, and finally – *finally* – gotten her first book deal at twenty-nine. Eight years later, she was finally making enough money from her ghost stories to quit her other job, fix up the camper that had been sitting in her garage ever since her father had passed, and take it wherever she damn well pleased.

And that was what she'd done, for the past six months. Rachel had spent a week or two finishing her fourth novel, Bunker, before setting off in the camper for Glasgow. Here, she'd stopped and begun work on a short story that she'd dreamed up on the drive, and found that the change of scenery fired up her imagination like nothing else had. She'd stayed in Glasgow for a week, and when she grew tired of the days writing and nights drinking, she moved on. She drove farther – into England, and to Cambridge – and spent almost a month working on the beginnings of her fifth novel (a sequel to her first, and a book that had so far eluded her, tentatively titled The Guest Returns) before driving on again. She stopped in laybys and pitched up on campsites, working outside at her little fold-up desk unless the weather demanded that she return to the shelter of the van; she lived cheap, hardly on-grid but always close enough to a bar, and worked hard while her agent perused the fourth book and the royalties from the first three filtered slowly into her account.

And this was the way it was. She had gone from place to place for a while, moving on only when the inspiration and the novelty of somewhere new became the drudgery of everyday. She had been headed for the Norfolk coast when she'd stumbled upon a news feature about some wild animal loose on the clifftops; a huge, carnivorous bird, they seemed to think, escaped from some psycho's private zoo. While that sounded interesting enough, she had figured this was as good a time as any to return home. Mother was pleased to see her, and she pitched up the van a few streets from her old apartment and stayed awhile.

Then she'd started to itch again, to crawl for the road, and so she'd said her goodbyes and headed for Wales. The Guest Returns was finally finished, and Bunker was due to hit shelves in a few weeks, and as much as she loved spending time with her mother, she needed to keep writing if she was to justify leaving her "real" job, and book six just... wasn't coming.

Sometimes, they didn't.

A change of scene would fix that.

She changed quickly, googling the nearest bar (she fancied pub food, rather than the pastries and barbecue meat she'd picked up from Ross-on-Wye – and, of course, she preferred to use the camper's little custom-built toilet as sparsely as possible) before sitting in the driver's seat and poring through the pages she'd typed out in the afternoon. Crossing through lines in her red pen and making a few small changes, she returned to the first page and scrawled cautiously across the top:

In the Pale Hills.

She almost smiled, ideas already trickling into her head for chapter two, chapter three – oh, and that ending – then she twisted the key in the ignition and her eyes moved to the dashboard as the display lit up. Almost seven, the dash clock told her.

She couldn't drive after three beers – shouldn't, at least – and it looked like about half an hour's walk to the nearest bar. Might as well leave and get some food before the kitchen staff reached the point where every new customer was just another set of dishes to wash before they could go home.

Turning off the engine and slipping the keys into her pocket, Rachel pulled her blood-red jacket on over her jumper and reached up into a small cabinet above the sleeping area, removing a thin wedge of cash and tucking it into her jacket.

She stepped out of the van and onto the road, looking about to make sure nobody had spotted the van and was writing her up a ticket. No, it was fine: she hardly expected there were many police patrols along this road, and besides, there was no sign. Not anymore.

Satisfied, she locked the camper behind her and started to walk in the direction of the bar, her steps clipping the rolling tarmac as she moved in the shadow of the Black Mountains.

25

<u>Chapter Three</u>
THE BEAST OF THE
BLACK MOUNTAINS

It was almost dark when Rachel reached the Lamplight Inn. The walk had taken a little over forty minutes – for that, she blamed her lack of familiarity with the steep hills around here – and by the time she came to a crooked, dimly-lit sign announcing her arrival at the public house, the sun had already begun to set behind the Black Mountains behind her, tendrils of light spilling across cloudy peaks and splashing the tops of each with gold and pink.

The sign jutted from an overgrown verge of privet hedging and, ducking beneath a low, green archway, she found herself on a small bridge. Just wide enough for a single car, the bridge sloped up across a narrow stream of tumbling river and looped around the back of the building on the other side. The inn itself stood at the top of another green, grassy slope where wooden picnic benches had been laid out haphazardly, some of their legs atop stubby concrete blocks so that all the table surfaces were level. The little sloping beer garden was pretty in the fading sunlight; strung up with tealights that blinked softly between the posts they were hung from, Rachel thought it might just be nice to sit out here overlooking the river and watch the last of the light die out.

The inn itself, she observed as she crossed the narrow bridge, was a quiet, thatched affair with white walls and wide windows lit amber from inside. Beneath each was a window-box stuffed with spring pansies and primroses, and the floral scent as she passed almost equalled the strong, hoppy smell from inside.

She walked to the gravel driveway and around the back of the pub, looking for the door; she found it nestled between two stone pillars, from which two burning lamps dangled on black chains. Around this side of the building, a crooked fire escape led to the second storey – accommodation, she supposed – and looking up, she saw a small, white cat sitting at the very top of the metal stairs and watching her.

'Hello, beautiful,' she whispered, offering up her hand and beckoning the cat down. It didn't move, and she shrugged. 'I'll catch you later, then.'

As she moved for the door, she caught sight of a pale blue Ford Orion parked across the driveway. Beside it, a white van with an '06 plate and, just a couple of spaces over, a silver Mercedes-Benz A-Class. The beaten up Orion looked even more beaten beside the sparkling, sleek Mercedes, and she noticed now that the undercarriages of both were streaked with dirt, though the Mercedes; indeed, she could feel the muck that had gathered on her boots and the ankles of her corduroys just from walking down here.

Rachel pushed open the door and stepped inside.

From within a narrow vestibule, the walls of which were all crumbling brickwork and candles jammed into rusted brackets, she could see right into the bar: a marbled wooden counter was scattered with damp beer cloths and, behind it, racks upon racks of bottles and glasses glimmered in all shining shades of blue and green as a scrawny bartender worked the taps. An elderly man sat beside a lit fireplace to the left; a second, younger man – dressed in a plaid shirt and crisp, tweed jacket – occupied a stool at the bar, and to her right, a young couple talked quietly over a game of cards. Rachel smelled hot pie and beer and stepped inside, pleasantly greeted with a warm wash of heat. The crackling of logs in the fire rippled softly across the restaurant.

The bartender looked up, cast her a nod without smiling. He was in his mid-twenties, she guessed, smart in plain white shirtsleeves rolled to his elbows and a neat, red waistcoat. She approached him, unease growing steadily in her belly as she felt the elderly patron's gaze on her back. She glanced briefly in his direction; in the amber light of the hearth, his furrowed brows tossed angry shadows into rheumy, green eyes and the frown lines across his forehead were deep and sunk into the skin. He watched her without expression, but she saw buried deep in those firelit eyes a terrible, burnt-out sadness and knew that he was far, far older than his years.

'What can I get you, my love?' said the bartender as she laid her hands on the wood and peered up into the racks.

'Hi,' she said, 'are you still serving food?'

'Sure I can get the kitchen staff to hang around a little longer,' he said. 'We're out of fish.'

'That's all right,' Rachel smiled. 'I'm more of a meat girl.'

'We're out of meat,' the bartender said flatly.

Rachel's face fell. 'Oh, okay. I—'

'No, I'm having you on,' he grinned, waving his hand. His accent was pleasant: thick and soothing and soft, curling around each word. 'Steak, roast beef – I'll get you a menu. You take a seat, wherever you like, my love. Fancy a drink?'

'Pint of your local, if you would.'

'Got a Wye Valley or a Motley Hog, love.'

Rachel smiled. 'Let's have a Hog, then, please.'

'On it.'

As he turned his back, Rachel said, 'Are you all right if I take a seat outside, out by the river?'

'I wouldn't,' came a hoarse, grumbling voice from behind her.

Rachel cocked an eyebrow, turning her head to look in the direction of the old man who'd spoken. He was hunched over the little round table by the fireplace, his neck and shoulders swallowed by the stiff collar of a thick, green coat. A near-finished pint of something dark and chewy sat before him on the table. 'And why's that?' Rachel said.

The old man shrugged. 'Gets real cold out there, real quick. Sun's set. Cold's coming.'

Rachel paused, then after a moment, nodded her agreement. 'Fair enough,' she said, turning back to the bar. She thanked the bartender for her pint and plucked a menu from the tray on the counter surface before moving away from the bar and toward a table in the corner. She nodded politely at the card-playing couple as she passed. They were already slipping on coats and clearing up after themselves as she sat down, so she wasn't offended when they left moments later, ferrying their empty plates to the bar and saying their goodbyes before ducking quietly out through the vestibule where Rachel had come in.

That left her, the bartender, and the old man by the fire. The younger man at the bar still hadn't said anything, and now she saw that he was scribbling on some yellowed paperwork over a half-pint of pale ale.

'Must have been something I said,' Rachel called across the restaurant as she sat, nodding toward the now-empty table.

The old man grunted.

'Let me guess, cold's coming?'

'Something like that.'

Rachel looked down and pored quickly through the menu. She was tempted by the steak, though the mushroom and stilton sauce sounded far too fancy for her appetite. Minutes later the bartender came to her table and she ordered a beef pie with veg and gravy. As he disappeared into the kitchen, she looked around. The walls were painted a stony shade of magnolia and lit in patches where candles jutted from the plaster on curled brackets. Above the fireplace, a wooden mantelpiece lay slightly crooked, and upon it framed photographs in grainy black-and-white were propped up either side of a short stack of crossword and puzzle books. The hearth itself popped and wheezed as thick logs burned brightly, and the warmth reached her even here. The opposite end of the room – she had to crook her neck to look back – drunken wooden beams careened through the wall, and hanging from hooks screwed into the wood were a selection of lit lanterns, each casting a pool of light in a different shade of amber. A small shelf was adorned with more books and board games; taking a quick drink, Rachel stood and moved to the shelf, picking through them until she found a battered travel guide. Hiking trails through the Black Mountains.

'May as well,' she murmured, taking the book back to her table and flicking it open.

She drank as she read, carefully storing maps in her memory and planning routes in her head. She couldn't write twenty-four hours a day, after all, and perhaps a good long hike into the hills would give her some inspiration.

She paused at the sound of shuffling footsteps, looked up expecting to see the bartender back with her food already. Instead, she saw the elderly man standing above her, the angry shadows on his face no less angry now that he'd moved away from the flickering firelight. He held two full pint glasses, one in each hand. He offered her one, and she beckoned to the chair across from her with a smile.

He sat, slid the beer across the table to her, and took a long, slow drink from his own. Then he swallowed, shook his head, and jabbed the travel guide with his finger. 'Don't,' he said.

Rachel frowned. 'What?'

'The Black Mountains,' he said, taking another drink. 'Don't go up there. Specially not when the sun's low.'

'Because of the cold?'

'Because of the Beast.'

Rachel heard a groan from the bar and looked up. The younger man in the tweed jacket – she supposed he must have been about forty or forty-five – turned to face them, smiling thinly. 'Don't let the old man spin his shit on you,' he said, 'there's no *Beast*. Not in the Mountains, anyway.'

Rachel cast a smile in the younger man's direction and turned back to the old man at her table. 'What are you talking about?'

'Been up there for twenty-five years,' the old man said. All the anger in his face was gone – if it had ever been there at all, and not just a projection of the firelight – and now all she saw was that deep well of sadness in his eyes. 'First came down to the village in ninety-six. Far as I know. It came down from the Mountains in the night and drained some poor farmer's goats of all their blood. Left their bodies scattered across the field, insides on their outsides.

'Now, this farmer thought that was the end of it, that some foul thing had gotten into the field and that was all. But the next night, the Beast returned. Took half his sheep. The third night, it took the rest of them. Drained of blood, bodies left strewn in the grass.

'Over the next few weeks, the Beast came down from the Mountains at night – every night – and picked off the livestock of all the farmers around, one by one. We found sheep in the fields, cows mutilated, lying on their sides, all drained of blood. Barn security couldn't keep it out – thing tore through padlocks and wood like paper and leaves.

'Years passed, and we turned to agriculture. No sense trying to raise livestock when there's something about like that that'll steal it off you. Thought it might get hungry, then, start coming after people, but it's not come down from the Mountains since.'

Rachel frowned. 'So how do you know it's still up there?'

The old man smiled sadly. 'People go up there, and they don't come back.'

Rachel's blood ran cold.

'The Beast was greedy, to begin with. It took

everything it could get. Now, it stays up in the hills and takes what is given to it, and for that, at least, we can be thankful. But people go missing in the Black Mountains, all the time. And it's the Beast what takes them.'

'Bollocks,' the younger man piped up.

Rachel looked up to see that he'd turned in his stool and was facing them, shaking his head.

'People go missing in the Mountains,' he said, 'but only the ones who get lost. There've been some terrible accidents up there over the years, but you'd be foolish for expecting otherwise. And those who get lost usually make their way back down eventually – we just don't hear about it. Why would we?'

Rachel shook her head. 'What do you mean?'

'Loved ones, family members, all make a fuss when someone goes missing. But the moment they come back, it's mouths shut, doors locked. Why shout about that? They don't need anyone to know someone's okay, only that they're not.'

'Fair enough.'

'It's the Beast,' the old man argued. 'You know how I know?'

Rachel shook her head.

'Because it was my goats he took first,' the old man said. Rachel's eyes were still on the man at the bar, and she watched as he silently mouthed those eight words in perfect time. He had heard this story before, a million times. And that was all it was, Rachel supposed. A story.

At the bar, the younger man shook his head and returned to his paperwork.

'You ever seen it?' Rachel asked the old man, taking a drink from the glass he'd bought her. 'The Beast?'

'I know folks that have,' the old man said. 'Folks that say it's as big as a bear, but built like a dog. Spikes all along its back. No fur, just leathery, wet skin. And claws, too, claws like the blades of a harvester.'

'Folks that have seen it and lived?'

The old man shrugged. 'All you need to know is those mountains ain't safe,' he said, finishing his drink and standing from the table. 'And you oughtn't go looking for danger up there.'

'Understood,' Rachel nodded. 'Thanks for the warning.'

He nodded, returned to his old table, and grabbed the thick, red scarf he'd left draped across a chair. With a curt goodbye to the younger man at the bar, he headed for the door and left.

Rachel drank quickly, and when her food came, she ate in silence. At the bar, the younger man finished poring through his documents and tucked them into a leather messenger bag at his waist. Thanking the bartender, he made to leave.

Passing by Rachel's table, he beckoned to the door. 'Where are you staying?' he said. 'I can drive you back, if you'd rather not walk in the dark.'

'Oh, that's all right,' Rachel smiled. 'Thank you. If the Beast gets me, at least you'll know it was all true.'

'Oh, I used to believe it,' the man said. 'Thought it was a vampire, when I first saw what had happened. But… it was the nineties. Lot of mad bastards at the time thought it'd be funny to mutilate animals like that. Wasn't ever a beast – just some pillock with a butcher knife and a dreadful sense of humour.'

'Sounds about right,' Rachel said, smiling thinly. There was something about this man – though friendlier, more personable – that seemed off. A radiance coming off him that told her, louder than the old man's words could, *stay away from those mountains*. 'What happened? Why'd you stop believing in it?'

'Grew up,' the man said. He held out his hand. 'Adrian, by the way.'

Rachel took it, shook briskly. 'Rachel.'

'You've got to move on, see. Gwynne – Gwynne

Lewis, that's the old fella – has been warning people away from the hills for years. Hasn't thought about getting livestock in his fields for longer.'

'But you've moved on?'

'People go missing, but people go missing all the time, everywhere. If there's any monsters round these parts, they're not coming after my sheep.'

'Thought there weren't any sheep around here anymore?'

Adrian lifted his hands and Rachel caught sight of the paperwork he'd been filling in at the bar. 'My father passed away a few weeks ago.'

'I'm sorry to hear that.'

'Me too. Thank you. Anyhow, his farm's been passed down to yours truly. Long time coming. And we're putting some sheep in those fields. Truck's coming tomorrow.'

'I see,' Rachel said quietly.

'Staying round here long?'

'Until the monster gets me, I guess,' she said.

Adrian cocked a smile, slipped a grey flatcap out of his jacket and onto his head, and called a goodbye to the bartender as he stepped out of the door.

Rachel left the Lamplight Inn a little after nine, thanking the bartender and tucking the travel guide into her pocket, promising she'd bring it back the next night. She almost expected him to give her his own account of the Beast of the Black Mountains, but he remained silent on the issue.

It was almost dark outside, but the last of the pinkish sunlight blossomed slowly across the horizon like spongy tissue. Crests highlighted white by that fading afterglow, the Mountains looked like they'd been scratched out of an oil painting, a thick palette knife carving black and white smears from the purple and gold of the sunset.

Looking across the driveway, she saw that the blue Orion and the sparkling, silver Mercedes had both gone, leaving the white van – presumably the bartender's – parked alone on the gravel.

Odd, she thought, that both men had driven home despite their half-drunk states. She prayed she wouldn't encounter either car lodged and broken in a ditch on her way back to the camper.

As she walked, she kept her eyes on the Black Mountains, peering up toward the tallest peaks as a stiff, aching pain rippled up her legs. The climb back up the road was steep and awkward but her mind was on other things.

She reached the T1 without incident – no crashed cars, and no monsters – and just as the night sky turned a calm, dark blue. Moonlight slid down the mountainsides and painted the fields in shades of steely grey. She looked out to the Black Mountains and smiled.

She had never paid warnings much mind.

Chapter Four
SHADOW

'Come on!' Haley yelled, tumbling up the path, almost tripping over her trainers as the rubbery soles scuffed hard earth and chipped fragments of stone. Around her the fringed silhouette of the long grass was a whistling blanket of thin, needle-like teeth. Far below the Black Mountains, her family were asleep.

'Hold up!' Andy called out somewhere behind her. 'I'm not – damn it – I'm drunk, Haley!'

'Me too,' she whooped, turning around and jogging backward up the path. Her hoodie fluttered around her in the wind, an empty can poking out of the pocket. The laces of her left shoe were undone. 'Come on, you two! We're nearly at the top!'

Andy glanced back, saw Rupert coming up clumsily behind him. 'Why did we let her drag us into this?'

Rupert yelled back something unintelligible, almost falling over and dropping into a spidery crawl up the slope. His hair was in his eyes and his glasses were crooked. He had vomited halfway up the mountain and he could still taste it in his mouth.

The moon was tinged with red above them, its edges splashed with blood. Andy couldn't help but avert his gaze, looking up ahead at the craggy mountain peak before them. The clouds that hugged the mountaintop were bruised and pinkish.

Red sky at night, he thought. How does the rest go?

'Come *on*!' Haley shouted, nearly at the top now. She wheeled around again, her body keening drunkenly. The old fuck at the Lamplight hadn't let them in – he'd quizzed them on the legitimacy of their IDs so many times that Andy was pretty sure he'd memorised each of their birthdays now – so they had grabbed a few cans at the corner shop and drunk them on their way up to the Mountains. Haley had drunk most of it, anyway. Andy wasn't about to admit that he was a lightweight, but he had been buzzing by the middle of the first can and downright pissed by the end of the second.

Everything was a little blurry, but he could make out her shape in the faint red glow of the moon, dancing clumsily across the path. He was going to kiss her when they reached the top. He had decided. Just now, actually. As soon as he was certain Rupert was out of the equation – the vomit had taken care of that – he had decided.

He hoped she would kiss him back.

Actually, speaking of Rupert…

Andy turned his head to look back again. 'Hey, Ru, keep up would you?'

He looked into the thick grass for their friend, pausing when he realised he had lost him. He glanced back to make sure Haley was still there – she was – then turned to peer more closely into the bushes canting down the slope.

'Rupert, buddy?'

Andy listened for retching, but heard nothing. Damn it, Rupert had fallen somewhere. He'd have to go back for him, now. That kiss was going to have to wait.

'Haley, Rupert's down! Let me just go pick him up…'

'What?' Haley yelled from up the hill, just as Andy had begun to stumble down the slope again. He huffed, turning round to face her, and opened his mouth to shout back—

And froze as he saw the dark shape slinking toward Haley from behind. His eyes widened.

The thing snatched her into the bushes before he

could scream her name. Haley was there one moment and whipped into nothingness the next. There was a horrific shriek and a spray of black pattered onto the path, and then Andy was running toward her, heaving his legs up the hill, Rupert all but forgotten, nothing but Haley on his mind, Haley and the hunched black shape that had rent her out of existence.

'Haley, hold on!' he cried drunkenly, belching as he ran. He stumbled, tripped, fell onto his face in the dirt. Scrambling to his feet, he called out again: 'Haley, wait, I'm coming—'

The shape stepped out onto the path in front of him, its enormous bulk silhouetted by the blood-red moon.

Andy screamed.

<u>Chapter Five</u>
A PREFERENCE FOR GOAT

Adrian Hyde woke to the sound of frantic knocking at the door. He grumbled, rolling over to check the old analogue alarm clock on the bedside cabinet. Just after four. He turned off the alarm that wouldn't go off for another half-hour and climbed groggily out of bed, yawning into his hand and clawing at the day-old stubble on his jaw.

The stairs groaned as he made his way downstairs. The old farmhouse still felt empty, felt soulless, and he had to believe that it was the absence of his father that had made it this way; either that or it was his own presence, and the idea that that might be the case chilled him a little. Did the house remember his father so fondly that the thought of anybody else – even the next in line, the heir to the throne that was the beaten-up Case 1056XL tractor out by the barn – stepping into his shoes was an imposter? He certainly felt like one, and he didn't need the cold drafts and strained floorboards to remind him.

'Coming, for Christ's sake,' he murmured, crossing the wide hallway to the front door as the hammering continued. He saw a hunched, grey shadow through the frosted glass of the door and groaned, twisting the handle to open it.

Gwynne Lewis stood on the doorstep, age never clearer on his face than when the early-morning sunlight picked at the lines across it and glinted like copper in his dull eyes. While Adrian was still dressed in the t-shirt and pyjama bottoms he'd slept in, Lewis had clearly been up for a while: he wore brown corduroys that were already splashed with mud, a green jacket bunched up at his chest, and grey wool gloves on his hands. Thin, white hair blew about his crooked face in the wind.

'Gwynne, please, not again—'

'Listen to me, boy,' Lewis said quietly, 'you can't. Please. You know it's a bad idea.'

Boy. The word spun round his head on a rinse cycle. 'Gwynne, that's enough. How many times do I have to tell you, this is just the way—'

'It'll get them,' Lewis said.

Adrian gritted his teeth. 'Remember when we had

this conversation twenty-five years ago?' he said. 'Remember when I was the scared little boy, and you were so... god, so wise and condescending—'

'I don't remember,' Lewis said.

'Well, you wouldn't,' Adrian said, 'would you, old timer? Christ, look me in the eyes and tell me you remember having this exact conversation yesterday.'

'I—'

'Yeah, don't bother,' Adrian said, pushing the door closed.

A wellington boot smacked the wood and it flew back into Adrian's hand. He saw red. 'Don't do it,' Lewis said. 'You put sheep in those fields, you're practically offering the damn thing an invitation to come down from the Mountains again.'

'Oh, the Beast?' Adrian smirked. 'Fuck off, Gwynne.'

'You know it's out there. You know it'll come back. The second it gets their scent on the wind.'

'Gwynne, enough.'

'It was always fonder of animal meat,' Lewis said quietly. 'You know as well as I do that it's only surviving on the human flesh it can scrape off the poor souls who go missing up there because there aren't any livestock around—'

'Good Christ, Gwynne! Enough! Listen to

yourself, for fuck's sake! "Human flesh"? Jesus, are you sick?'

'Adrian, listen to me. Please. No sheep. It'll take them.'

'If there truly is a beast out there – and if it's the same thing that killed your livestock—'

'—and your father's—'

'—and my father's, in ninety-six, then my sheep'll be just fine.' He grinned sardonically. 'You know whatever that thing was had a preference for goat, anyway.'

Lewis opened his mouth.

Adrian got there first. 'Leave it alone, old man,' he said, shaking his head sadly. 'Times have changed. Things around here have to change with them, especially if that means going back to the way we should have been doing it all along.'

'Times haven't changed for *shit*,' Lewis spat, 'not in the ways that matter. Only thing changing round here is farms getting taken over by people who wouldn't know a ewe from a nanny 'less either one started chewing his—'

'Gwynne, get off my doorstep,' Adrian said calmly, his voice leaden with fury. 'Get off my farm.'

'Ain't your farm, boy,' Lewis said. 'It's your daddy's. It'll always be your daddy's—'

'I said get *off*,' Adrian said, stepping out through the open door and shoving Lewis hard in the chest. The old man stumbled back, tripping on the step beneath him and staggering back into the wet earth. Lewis grunted, righted himself, but Adrian was still coming, nostrils flaring as anger flashed in his eyes. 'You get off my farm and you don't come back, you horrible little man.'

'Adrian, listen…'

'I've listened long enough,' Adrian snarled, storming forward as the hunched old man backed away from him. The younger man's fists were clenched, his knuckles so white they looked as if they might pop. His teeth ground together as he spoke. 'You get away from me and don't ever fucking come back here again, Lewis.'

The old man shook his head as he backed away, stumbling across the slarry driveway. 'It'll come, boy. It'll come for them.'

'We'll see,' Adrian said, 'now fuck off, old man.'

Lewis threw one last, pleading look in Adrian's direction, sadness biting at the corners of his eyes and twisting his face in knots. Then he turned to go, heading for the battered Orion parked at the edge of the drive.

Adrian flexed his fingers, anger throbbing hot and thick through his blood. He watched the little blue car reverse down the track to the road and disappear.

'Fucking shithead,' Adrian muttered, then he turned back and headed inside. The door slammed closed.

Sunlight beat through the camper's windscreen and splashed Rachel's tiny mattress with shades of grey and purple. She woke and stretched, her feet curling off the edge of the crude sleeping area, then slowly rose and dressed. Yawning, she pulled on her UHI hoodie and jeans and made sure she had her keys in her pocket before stepping out of the T1. With the door still open, she checked her pocket again; and a third time once she'd shut it behind her. Worse things had happened than locking her keys inside the van, but she didn't particularly want to have to jimmy open the passenger door again. Especially not since doing so had revealed just how far from secure her living quarters were.

Rachel dug around in the storage trunk, pulling out her portable barbecue and a small bag of coal briquettes. She set both around the front of the van, where the sunlight had begun to gather in small, dappled pools on the tarmac. Propping up the barbecue on its little legs, she opened up the lid and lifted the grill to toss a few handfuls of coal inside.

Dipping into her pocket for matches, she lit the grille and went around back to pee.

While thin, greasy flames stroked the barbecue grille, she brought out the old blue typewriter and sat in the sunlight with the sour taste of smoke roiling on the air around her. After twenty minutes she had typed out a page and a half; she went back into the camper to brew some coffee and came out again to find the barbecue smouldering and ready to cook on.

Coal briquettes glowed white, thin waves of orange and amber flitting across each surface and melting into a little damp pool of light at the very base of the barbecue. The grill was warm; she held her palm above it and felt heat spill up between her fingers. Ripping open a packet of hash browns, she laid four across the grille and returned to the typewriter as they cooked.

Ghost stories came easy, and never easier than in the early-morning light with hash browns grilling less than four feet away. When she'd finished typing out a second page and fed the third into the machine, she flipped over the hash browns and buttered two slices of bread. In the Pale Hills could be her next bestseller. She pondered that as she slid the cooked hash browns into sandwiches and ate, looking up at the Black Mountains. But perhaps ghost stories had had their chance; perhaps she ought to move on, after this.

Maybe she'd write about monsters.

After breakfast, Rachel spent another two and a half hours writing before packing everything up in the camper and getting ready to head out. She considered replacing the No parking overnight sign she'd torn down overnight, but she hadn't seen a single vehicle come past all morning and she was half-convinced it had been equally desolate all night; there was no sense reserving a space for the camper, she thought, if there was no one around to steal it.

She drove the T1 toward the Black Mountains, hoping to find somewhere nearby to park up for the day while she explored. As she neared the hills their peaks seemed to stretch and tilt upward, plunging out of the ground and jutting up into the low clouds above. The Mountains were more green and brown, up close, than black: those steep slopes were driven through with rough pathways and walkways, and gorse and long grasses splashed them with colour. The sun was higher now and golden light spilled down the hills toward her as the fields and commons spread and widened. If not for the slopes and curves of the ground she'd have been able to see for miles; the fields were sparse and ruined, the heathland between them rough and ragged. A wasteland. Where deciduous trees had ruled in the summer, now they were barren, clawed spindles of black in the red-brown tangles of the thickets and bracken that anchored their pale, wormy roots to the ground. In places, and at the edges of fields, pine trees grew thick and green, but through the sunlit gaps between them Rachel just saw more grassland.

Not a sign of life around.

How hungry must the Beast of the Black Mountains be, if it lived off hikers and visitors? There *were* none.

She came to a turnoff and peeled the camper slowly around the corner, the van rumbling beneath her as tarmac became dirt and gravel crumbled into soft verges either side. The road was gone and the incline was steeper; she felt that she was in the Mountains already.

Rachel pulled the camper into a ragged passing place, mirrored on the other side of the narrow road by another, and turned off the engine. Climbing out, she pulled on the jacket she'd slung over the passenger seat and breathed in the cool air. She checked – twice – that she had her mobile, keys, and the pocket-knife she had dug out of the glovebox, and then she checked a third time to be sure. There wasn't really a Beast up there, she knew that, but she was sure the old man had been right about something: people had gone missing up here. It happened. Hikers got lost, or bogged down… and she was certain that many of them had turned up safe and sound with no great trauma attached to their extended walk – who would know? – but either way, she wouldn't be one of those people. She had the GPS on her phone – not to mention the ability to call someone if needed – and she wasn't going far, anyway.

She looked up into the hills and smiled. She felt a strange kind of exhaustion just peering up into the peaks, but it was the kind that warmed her, that made her bones feel solid and useful.

Dipping back inside the camper, Rachel grabbed two beers from the mini-fridge and slipped one into her jacket. The other, she held in one hand as she stepped back out of the T1 and locked it.

She checked the lock. Once, twice, three times.

Safe.

Bending down to pop the lid off the beer bottle on the wheel-arch of the van, she drank as she walked, heading along the path into the Mountains. The air was crisp and drew sharp fingers across her face as a soft, sticky wind made her eyes sting. She could hear babbling water somewhere nearby. As she wandered up the side of the mountain, the path dissolved and she found herself looking for traces of humanity in the barren expanse of green grass that covered the slope. For signs that people had been here before. At one point, it seemed, there had been a pathway, for the grass was an inch or two shorter than the rest where it cut through the middle. But it was a long time since anybody had hiked it; there were no footprints, and the soil beneath her feet was so much like clay that she was certain there would have been. Indeed, looking back she saw that she had made a path of her own, her heels churning out chunks of earth as she walked.

The ascent hadn't seemed particularly steep, but looking back she saw that the camper was a fair way beneath her; she must have been walking for half an hour, at least, and she could see farther across the fields than before. Looking down and following the road, she was amazed to see that the track to the Lamplight Inn was visible from here, that the road carved through the swelling fields like a long, grey ribbon laid flat upon the surface of the ocean and then tossed and twisted about when a wave came.

She kept climbing, enjoying the strain in her legs and the soft, lilting music of the wind around her. She let her mind wander, let herself drift into imagination and daydreaming. Within an hour she was ready to return to the camper and continue writing; scenes seemed to plot themselves out so clearly when she walked, games and players aligning in her mind until she could see a winner. She had often walked the streets of Inverness late at night, headphones on, soft music pouring into her, allowing herself to slip into that scape of muscle memory and liquid thought. That was when ideas came, when whole stories mapped themselves out in her head. That was when she could free herself.

She felt free now. The mountain around her was a cascade of gorse and plant-life; she smelled coconut on the wind and imagined it was the pollen of something nearby. Fragments of rock jutted from the ground, stepping stones scattered and broken to obscure the path they'd once made. She wondered how much of the debris had been brought up here, and how much had emerged from the mountain itself or tumbled down the slope from the very top—

She heard something. A crunch, the slight press of a heel on damp wood.

Rachel froze, halfway up the slope.

A shadow flitted across her vision and she looked up; a kestrel that had been hovering above her dived, suddenly, plummeting into the grass where it clawed at a tiny field vole. Talons dug in and the bird swung away on the wind, carrying its prey with it.

That was all, she thought. The sound had just been

an animal moving through the gorse, perhaps another vole or a mouse.

She walked on a little way, wary of any tiny sound. Her own footsteps seemed louder now, almost unbearably so, and her heartbeat pounded in her ears. The mountain seemed to be listening too, and she almost found herself hoping it would warn her of anything it heard before she did.

Don't be thick, she told herself. The old man's words were on her mind, but she knew that if he hadn't said anything, she would have paid no mind to the crunch of wood. Just an animal. She looked all around, into the thick tangles of gorse and the clawed structures that had once been trees and stumps. Nothing. Just an animal.

Just—

Behind her, something moved.

There was something following her.

<u>Chapter Six</u>
LIVESTOCK

Frozen in place, Rachel Wheatley listened to the crunch of bony feet in the dirt around her and the thumping of her own frantic heartbeat. Blood swelled in her veins as adrenaline juddered through her. Desperately she looked around, hardly daring to move her head but swinging her pupils into the corners of her eyes; nothing. Nothing around her but tall, wild grass, scattered, broken rocks, and clusters of thick, thorny deciduous hedging.

A shadow blotted out the sunlight peeling through one of the bushes to her left and disappeared again, leaving the shrub shot through with lamplit holes. She followed the direction of its movement with her eyes: nothing. It was gone again.

Staying as still as possible, Rachel slid her hand into her jeans and curled her fingers around the delicate, ivory handle of the pocket-knife.

Maybe there was nothing. Better safe than sorry.

She straightened up, satisfied that it – whatever it was – had gone, and continued to walk.

As she climbed, the thorny, sparse bushes around her grew higher and thicker so that soon ascending was like navigating a maze, the walls of which scratched and clawed at her calves. Further up, she could see a blanket of yellow-splashed gorse covering the mountainside; beyond that, though, the bushes dissipated and made way for an easier route of dirt and grass. Once she'd passed through this thorny minefield, the rest of the trip to the top would be—

Something skittered. Off to her right this time. Definite footsteps, the grinding of lithe hooves in the earth.

Rachel paused, glancing back the way she'd come. She could not see to the bottom of the hill – the slope curved to one side, and she was conscious that at some point she had almost turned a bend – but a glint of sunlight on metal told her that the camper was down there somewhere, at least.

Turn back, whispered the voice in her head. Turn back *now*.

She kept climbing, struggling up a narrow path through the bushes toward the gorse that she knew would dig and tear at her ankles. Once she was through all that, she was *through*, and onto the home stretch.

If it doesn't get you first.

'Nothing out here,' she whispered to herself, swiping at the arms of a bush that bunched together and scraped at her hip. And she was right, surely; she felt confident that whatever she'd heard was just a badger or a bird. Something normal, something safe. Not something that had made its lair up here…

On her left, ragged breathing. Another step. An animal larger than a badger. Her head snapped to the side and she caught a glimpse: pale fur, black skin raked over its face, shining yellow eyes. Her heart stopped in her chest and she stepped back, wincing as thorns pressed into her heel and dug thin, warm welts up her shin.

The shape was gone, but she could still hear it. Stepping carefully between the bushes, its breathing ripping streaks from the air. There was a strange tension on the air, as though the creature were more afraid of her than she was of it. A stretch, she thought, or plain old wishful thinking.

Did it know she was there? Was it hunting her, or had she strayed into its territory?

She backed up slowly, keeping her eyes on the sunlit hedges, scanning for any sign of movement beyond them. More thorns at her back. She looked down, saw an opening in the bushes behind her. Quickly, she scrambled through it, ducking to hide amongst them.

She crouched in the dirt, her shoulders and back raked by the spiny branches as she breathed shallow, quiet breaths, hardly daring to move.

The creature appeared in the walkway, standing just a few yards from where she'd been moments ago. She couldn't truly see it through the tangle of thorns across her field of view but she saw shapes: stubby, black legs ending in blood-smeared hooves. Ears twitching, face contorted into a snarl with black lips peeled back from tombstone teeth.

It sniffed and pawed at the air, snuffling toward her. No, she thought, god, no, don't let it find me… She clawed at the dirt beneath her and found a stone, a slim shaft of flint in the shape of an arrowhead. Curling her fingers around it, she raised her arm, gently, slowly – and cast the stone away, tossing it into the shrubs the other side of the path.

There was a brittle crack! as the thing soared through thin, bare branches and skittered into the dirt.

The creature whirled around, peeling toward the sound, and Rachel took her chance, staggering to her feet and plunging out from behind the bushes, wheeling back the way she'd come. Forget the top now, head back for the camper, for safety—

She had barely made it a few steps when the creature reared up in front of her, barrelling out of the thickets and bleating madly in her face. It kicked up its hooves and clouds of dirt flew up around them as it screamed, wailing into the air—

Her mouth opened, but no words came.

Relief flooded her body.

It was a ewe.

A plump, freshly-sheared sheep with trim, white wool and leathery folds rippling across its face. Its black lips were rubbery and blistered and as it moaned harshly its yellowed teeth clashed together.

Rachel raised her arms to calm the animal but it was in distress, its yellow eyes wild and round and terrified. Its ears twitched as if batting away flies and it backed away, suddenly afraid of *her* now that she was right in front of it.

'It's okay,' she whispered, still frightened of the animal – frightened that it might kick her in its panic, or tumble over and hurt itself on the rocks. 'Hey, it's okay, stop that, it's okay…'

The ewe backed up. She finally registered that it was spattered, covered with blood, deep red pools spreading and seeping through its rigid woollen coat. Four deep gashes across its chest – four claw marks raking it open – oozed crimson and flung gluey strings of it into the ground. One of its yellow eyes was clouded with red, and there were more claw marks rending its dark face open.

Something had attacked it.

This wasn't the creature, no, but what if there was something else out there?

About thirty minutes before Rachel Wheatley pricked her heel on a knot of thorns in the hills, the long, rattling bulk of a truck came barrelling down the road just a mile from her camper, a truck carrying sixty-five sheep destined for a three-point-five-acre field that had specially, deliberately been allowed to grow wild and unkempt on Adrian Hyde's land.

Phil Rees was listening to Springsteen's *Jungleland* and belting along at full volume, both cab windows rolled all the way down so that the wind buffeted the driver's face and chest. A rusted fan rattled on the dash, its blades clack-clack-clacking as they spun. He'd have turned it off, but all that noise and chaos – the music, the wind, the constant smack of metal on metal – drowned out the agonising wails of the sheep in the back of the lorry.

He always thought they sounded strangled, bleating back there, as though tight ribbons of razor wire had been wound through the partitions in the semitrailer and around their necks.

The speakers throbbed and crackled, almost at their limit, as Bruce ripped a last, crashing heartache of a chorus over backing music that bled and ran red with passion. Phil Rees howled along with it, rapping his palms on the wheel as he cruised the truck along a downward-sloping road, peeling to the right and curving left again. Guiding the lorry, rather than steering it. He'd done these roads too many times to take their eerie emptiness for granted; even with all that noise, he was focused, pinned on the tarmac ahead and always, always looking for the next bend. And all the while, the animals in the back stumbled and bumped each other, peering out through thin, rectangular slits in the semitrailer walls at the rolling, swelling hills around them.

Phil turned down the stereo as he came around a tight, stiff corner and immediately he heard them in the back: screaming, pleading in that awful wailing language of theirs, bleating and moaning for freedom. Nearly there, he thought, peering ahead for any sign of oncoming traffic. Nearly—

A shadow darted into the road and reared up in front of the cab, flashes of white and red glancing across its back. Phil's eyes widened as his steel toe-capped boot slammed into the brake. The creature stood unfazed in the dim side-lights of the lorry, snarling up at him. He barely had time to register the thing's leathery hide, the spines along its back, before he caught sight of the bone white teeth and realised it was leaping for the windscreen.

Phil yanked the wheel down hard and the lorry keened over to the other side of the road. A flash of something huge filled the window as the thing overshot, and he heard the smack of clawed paws on the tarmac as it landed somewhere out of his field of view. He tried to correct the lorry, to steer it back on course, but now his grinding foot on the brake was having some effect and the tyres screamed in protest.

In seconds, he was beached.

The lorry lay across the road, still save for the drunken swaying of the semitrailer as it settled on the undercarriage. Phil Rees jabbed a button on the dash and Springsteen fell immediately silent, the eerie quiet filling the cab. The rattling fan blades smacked at each other in time with his pounding heart: *tk-tk-tk-tk-tk-tk*. The sheep in the back had stopped bleating, and somehow their silence was worse than their constant wails. They were waiting, just as frightened as he was – except he had seen it, he had seen that terrible creature in the road and he knew that it couldn't have just disappeared...

Drawing in a deep breath, he calmed himself, laid

a hand on the gearstick, and prepared to right the truck and get going again.

The grinding of bone on metal made him freeze, his knuckles whitening on the knob. A long, awful scream of rending plastic and steel carried through the cab. And the sheep started bleating again, their moans louder and more shredded than before. The clatter of something thrown to the tarmac and now the semitrailer was rocking, bobbing on the propshaft, the rear axle straining loudly.

'What the…'

Phil mashed at his seatbelt, finally popping it open, and fumbled with the driver's side door. In the wing mirror he caught a glimpse, a flash of something flung into the road. And he saw a single ewe, standing on the tarmac at the rear end of the lorry. Too scared to run.

Something splashed the ewe's face with red and a low bleat turned to a shriek of pain and Phil tumbled out of the cab and staggered along the road toward the back of the lorry and stopped and bent and *saw* it—

Jesus Christ, he could see it all.

He stood at the back of the semitrailer and looked in as terrified sheep filtered out of the carriage through a mangled, rent-open hole in the back. They trotted past him, away from him, leaving him to gape into the dark of the truck.

A plump ewe stood at the lip of gouged metal, as if considering her options. She stared at him, eyes wide and wet. Made as if to step out and onto the road—

And something dragged her back in, hooves smacking the bed of the lorry. Phil winced at another scream.

'Hey!' Phil yelled, stepping up and fumbling for the flashlight in his jacket pocket. He clicked it on and swung the beam up into the dark of the semitrailer.

The creature looked up at him, grinning, ribbons of blood and drool hanging from its leathery maw.

'*What* the…'

He watched helplessly as it plunged its claws into the ewe's chest and twisted, spraying another's face with blood. The poor animal kicked and struggled as the creature bent its snout into the opening, and there was an awful, wet slopping sound as it began to drain the ewe of blood.

Barely thinking, Phil threw the flashlight. The beam swung wildly around the walls of the trailer, briefly igniting dented sheets of metal with pale light; he saw pale, lifeless bodies thrown about, drained of colour, some still twitching. The butt of the flashlight smashed into the creature's shoulder and bounced off. It looked up, fury streaking its glinting eyes, and the ewe at its feet bucked, taking her opportunity to kick up with her hooves and strike it in the throat. It tipped back and the ewe struggled to her feet, the flashlight rolling across the floor as she trotted desperately for the open back of the lorry and tumbled out, running past him.

Phil watched as the creature rose from the dark, lean, muscular shoulders rippling wetly as the spines along its back quivered. Powerful legs drove it forward as it stalked toward him. Its mouth was red with blood, teeth like knives.

Something flashed silver at its neck.

The creature bared its teeth and came for him.

Rachel watched as the blood-spattered ewe turned and ran away, canting into the gorse farther up the hill and disappearing into a blanket of thick, leafless growth and carving up its hind legs as it vanished.

Heart still in her mouth, she stood there for a moment. The gouge marks across the animal's chest, the blood in its eyes…

Christ, the old man at the bar had been right. There was something out here.

Rachel steeled herself, drawing in breaths and letting them go, looking up to the mountain peak.

Not worth it, she thought. You've had your stubborn little adventure, haven't you? Get back down to the camper, drive away. You could go back to that quiet little layby and spend the afternoon working. Or you could drive right back across the border and leave this place behind.

Either way, she thought, you'll have to start walking.

Forcing herself to move, she turned away from the mountaintop and started back down the way she'd come. It was simultaneously easier going down than it had been coming up and more difficult: easier because gravity meant she didn't have to expend as much energy, but more difficult because the steepness of the descent meant that she had to angle her feet very carefully, and her legs were shaky enough already.

She walked cautiously through the rakish deciduous bushes and as they began to thin, caught sight of the T1 at the bottom of the hill.

Something glinted sharply to her right.

She paused, cocking her head to the side to peer into the shrubs there. For a moment she saw nothing, thought she must have imagined it.

Then as she turned her head back, she saw it again.

A tiny sliver of light in the corner of her eye,

bouncing off something glassy in the spiky undergrowth.

Slowly, she headed for the shrub, then as she neared she bent down to peer into the tangled thorns and twisted, knotted branches.

A camera was screwed to the base of the shrub.

A TrailCam decked out in camouflage paint, smeared with shades of green and yellow. The sunlight had glinted off a small, glass lens. Plastic rims were smeared with dirt.

'What…' Rachel whispered, reaching forward. A tiny red light blinked in the corner of the TrailCam's bulky framework. The thing was turned on. Watching.

Perhaps, if this was the lair of the creature she'd been warned about, then whoever had set this up had seen it.

Quickly, she moved around to the side of the camera and picked it open, using the thin edge of the blade of her pocket-knife to twist open the screws holding its casing together.

The camera swung open and she explored inside, finally finding the slot into which a tiny memory card had been pressed.

She removed it, slid the card into her pocket, and snapped the TrailCam shut again.

Standing, somewhat satisfied with her amateur

detective work, Rachel saw a slim, metal lockbox half buried in the dirt behind the shrub.

Frowning, she stepped around the thorny bush and bent down again, scraping away little clouds of earth until she'd revealed the rest of the lockbox. It was long, rectangular, painted a dull shade of brown so that it disappeared quite easily into the dirt.

It was padlocked. She tried to pick it, but with no luck.

Gingerly, she laid the box down in the earth and kicked, slamming her heel into the padlock. There was a metallic crack! but the padlock remained firm. She kicked again.

It sprung open and she leant down to flip open the lid of the lockbox, cocking an eyebrow at the contents.

A length of rope, coiled in on itself and knotted loosely into a frayed bundle.

A packet of cable ties, a roll of black waste-disposal bags, and a pocket-knife similar to her own.

And – finally – a sharp, red fire axe.

<u>Chapter Seven</u>
MEN IN BLACK

Rachel pulled the camper to the side of the road when she saw the flashing lights ahead. The police had turned off the sirens now but she saw two cars parked across the road, their noses tilted inward and almost nudging each other. Back behind the carnage, she saw a third.

The lorry had tipped over onto its side, batted by some incredible force so that its semitrailer had knocked loose massive chunks of earth from the verge at the roadside and ripped right through the laurel hedging. The windscreen of the cab was shattered and she saw great, stringy sheets of blood running through the grille.

The back of the truck was torn open, a mangled mess of steel and bloody, sheared edges. Thin clumps of wool fluttered on ragged corners like knots of white flag, waving weakly in the wind.

Rachel stepped out of the camper and moved slowly toward the barricade, careful not to get too close and ignite the attention of the two police officers on the roadside, both of them huddled over a long, shapeless lump smeared across the tarmac. She didn't want to get moved on; no, she wanted to *see.*

As she neared the blockade she saw Adrian Hyde standing near the back of the truck, his face pale. He ran a hand through his hair, staring into the mess of the inside of the trailer.

The old man from the bar – Gwynne Lewis – stood beside him, gazing into the same dark, blood-spattered space. Behind them, a third police officer scrawled messily in her pocketbook. Blue lights flashed and flickered and washed the whole scene in an unholy, pearlescent glare that pulsed and throbbed with Rachel's trembling heart.

Rivers of blue ran off the red in the road and the scent of copper and pennies rang like heady fumes in the thick, cobalt fog.

Peering over the nose of the nearest police car, Rachel saw what the two officers were huddled over. She balked. 'Oh, Christ…'

Behind the truck, Lewis raised a withered hand and laid it on Adrian's back. The younger man recoiled at the elder's touch; Rachel saw, in the corner of her eye, a flash of disgusted anger breach Adrian's otherwise pallid expression.

The old man withdrew his hand, saying something quiet to Adrian – were they words of comfort? – before pulling back from the younger man, stepping away to give him space. Lewis's face was a torn mess of emotion; Rachel had already guessed – from the wool and the blood, and from the carcasses sprawled through the hedge and the field beyond, the carcasses she hadn't dared spare a second glance – that this ill-fated lorry had been delivering Adrian's livestock, but the older man looked twice as upset that it had been turned over.

In fact, she thought, looking across at Adrian once again, the younger man hardly looked upset at all. What she had mistaken moments ago for a pallor of concern had twisted into a farcical, thin mask of feeling laid across a face that had already steeled itself. He was thinking, and thinking hard, and she could almost see the wheels turning behind his eyes, but he wasn't broken up.

She frowned. Moving away from Adrian, Gwynne Lewis looked away – into the field, toward those broken corpses – and she saw tears streaming slowly down his face. He walked toward the farthest police car and the officer raised her head to talk briefly with him. He seemed to answer a couple of questions as she wrote in her pocketbook, and then with a curt nod and a glance back in Adrian's direction, he moved past the car and disappeared.

Adrian Hyde stood motionless at the back of the lorry, wringing his flatcap in both hands.

Rachel looked back toward the officers nearest to her and saw that they'd begun to cover the body. The driver's face was a ghastly white, the skin so tight that it had bruised where it was sucked in to his cheekbones, the sockets around his rolled-up eyes black and blotchy. She saw a savage rip of blood-smeared flesh across his throat, and when she heard the *zzip* of the body-bag being sealed over his face she almost imagined the officer doing the zipping had begun at one end of the terrible gash in his neck and ended at the other.

'Terrible business,' came a voice from behind her shoulder.

Rachel turned, cocked an eyebrow as she saw Gwynne Lewis approaching. 'Wondered where you'd stalked off to,' she said.

'I was going to head home,' Lewis said, wiping his nose on his wrist as he stepped up beside her. 'Saw you across here and thought I'd come do you a favour.'

'What favour is that?'

'Tell you to turn round,' he said. 'You won't get past on this road, that's for sure, but… you ought to leave, either way. Get out of this place.'

'Is this your beast's work, then?' Rachel said quietly.

'Hardly *my* beast,' Lewis said, smiling sadly.

'You know what I mean.'

'I do. My point stands: whatever can do this to a lorry of that size… you and your camper need to get back across the border and far away from here.'

Rachel shook her head, looking up into the field behind the smashed semitrailer. Jauntily-angled legs poked up from broken rumps and drained, white bodies. 'You know,' she said quietly, 'the English used to cut off the ears of any Welshman who crossed the Dyke into England.'

'How times change.'

'And the Welsh… well, I think the Welsh used to hang any Englishman found west of it.'

'According to George Borrow, at least,' Lewis countered. 'Sometimes, it's all scare tactics. True or not, you can bet the English were more frightened of crossing over Offa's little wall than the Welsh were.'

'Exactly,' Rachel said. She turned to him. 'You're a storyteller, Mr. Lewis. "The Beast of the Black Mountains". Why are you trying to scare people away?'

'Look at what's in front of you,' Lewis said quietly. 'The more people I "scare away", the better.'

'Good point.'

Rachel heard the faint rumbling of an SUV engine and looked up to see a matte-black Volvo coming slowly around a bend in the road and pulling up beside the farthest police car. The officer with the pocketbook folded it into her pocket and glanced toward her colleagues before heading toward the car.

'Will he be all right?' Rachel said, nodding toward Adrian Hyde, who hadn't noticed the approaching SUV.

'He'll be fine,' Lewis said, almost bitterly. 'I spoke to him a moment ago. He's already thinking about claiming his insurance money.'

'He can do that?'

'Of course he can,' Lewis shrugged.

'He – wait, he said that to you?'

'I was speaking to him just a moment ago,' Lewis nodded. 'Little bastard. Came into his daddy's farm without any idea how it all works, and now… good lord, now this… I warned him. You know that? I warned him, but the selfish little…'

'Okay,' Rachel said. 'I'm sorry. I'm sure he was just trying to do his best for—'

'Maybe,' Lewis said. 'And now they're all dead.'

Rachel swallowed. She watched as three men

stepped out of the black Volvo, leaving the driver's seat empty. They were all dressed oddly like funeral directors. The first, and tallest, offered the police officer a leather bound ID and folded it back into his black blazer. A crisp, grey waistcoat hugged his torso. Behind him, the others – a broad-shouldered Black man and a grey haired shape in sunglasses – nodded in her direction and headed straight for the lorry.

'Who are they?' Rachel said.

'I don't know,' Lewis shook his head. 'Animal control?'

'Animal control in black suits and shades?'

'Well, depends on the animal, I suppose.'

Rachel almost smiled at that. 'Fair enough.' She frowned, remembering something. 'Hey, you remember last night, when you warned me about going up into the mountains?'

Lewis paled.

'Well, let's say I completely ignored your advice—'

'You didn't. Did you?'

'Maybe. Listen—'

'You stupid girl,' Lewis hissed, stepping up close. 'Do you know what could have happened to you up there?'

She looked at him, unease creeping suddenly

through her where, before, there had just been confusion and fear. 'Yes,' she said, nodding toward the scene before them. Two of the men in black had approached the police officers nearest to them and were relieving them of the body, which they carried – bag and all – toward the matte-black Volvo. The third had joined Adrian Hyde at the back of the lorry and was asking him something. 'Now, I do. I know what could've happened. But I didn't, before, and I went up there… and I found something.'

Lewis cocked an eyebrow. 'You did?'

'A TrailCam,' she said. She dug into her pocket and flashed him the little memory card before slipping it away again. 'Set up to watch the walkway.'

Lewis's face didn't change. 'Doesn't seem all that,' he said, shaking his head a little. 'People like to watch out for the wildlife.'

'Wildlife?'

'Yeah, you know… kites, buzzards. Field voles.'

'Field voles?'

'Among other things. Lots of badgers round here.'

'And all these things… they're up in the Black Mountains, just casually hanging out with a Beast that likes to murder livestock and drink blood?'

'Well, who knows how long that camera's been

up there?'

'Certainly not the twenty-five years that the Beast has. It was recent, I think. Hardly dirty at all. And still working – someone's been watching up there.'

Lewis nodded. 'Maybe.' He gestured toward the tallest of the men in black as he stepped into the wreck of the semitrailer, crouching to run his fingers across the bloody metal. 'Maybe it was these fellas.'

Rachel said nothing.

'Listen,' Lewis said quietly, stepping up behind her and laying a hand on her back. 'I'm sorry, I really am. I know you probably came up here to… well, to get away from it all, or for a little peace and quiet. And to be faced with all this… it's a nightmare.'

'You really think he'll be okay?' she said, nodding in Adrian's direction.

'He's lived here his whole life,' Lewis nodded. 'I'll do what I can for him – if he'll let me. He knows what to expect around here. I tried to… it doesn't matter. He knows where to find me, whatever he needs.'

'You're a good man,' Rachel said quietly.

'I try,' he smiled sardonically, patting her back gently. 'Anyway, I'll see you round. Or – hopefully, if you do what's good for you – I won't. Take care, sweetheart.'

She nodded, watching the men in black shut the

Volvo's door on the bagged cadaver as Lewis walked away.

The noon sun bled slowly into a sky that was peppered with the frail tips of semi-visible clouds, a sky that was all too blue for all the blood on the road.

Gwynne Lewis turned and begun to walk away from the awful scene on the tarmac, hands in his pockets. Poor Adrian and his sheep. It was all happening again…

But he'd warned him. He'd told that youngun how this would play out. The creature had been content with its feed, with the odd hiker and lost traveller – and Christ bless all their souls, poor buggers, for what had happened to them was truly awful – but to offer the thing a buffet, to tempt it back to the village…

It was almost a good thing this had happened, he thought, half convincing himself. At least now that sly young bastard wouldn't try anything like this again.

At least now he *knew* the danger.

Lewis set his jaw grimly, thumbing the thing in his pocket. He checked behind him before pulling it out, turned it over in his hand when he was sure nobody could see him.

The memory card was flecked with dust, but presumably still functional.

He slid it back into his pocket and kept walking.

Chapter Eight
MASTER

Navigating a series of ever-tightening side roads about the radius of the unholy collision, Rachel eventually managed to pull the camper back around to the quiet layby she'd found on her first day. She considered pausing for lunch, but found that her appetite had all but disappeared.

Bringing the portable desk and typewriter around to the back of the van, she spent a little while writing in the afternoon shade, but her mind was on blood and mutilated things and she could hardly think straight, let alone fire up an imagination that was already so solely occupied on something else. Both sides of her brain worked hard to remind her of the scattered bodies she'd seen in the hedgerow, torn limbs poking through ragged clumps of thorn, faces drained of colour – and of the cadaver of the driver, already half-bagged but still visible enough that she could see the pallor of his face, the awful gouged mess of his neck…

She remembered what Lewis had said the night before about missing people. Not many, he'd said, but it was inevitable that the odd hiker disappeared. And over the course of twenty-five years…

These half-thoughts and fancies were no good. She had to find something – even if not to get to the bottom of it all, then to at least plunge in a hand and dig around as deep as she could. Even if that meant getting that hand dirty, or caked in blood.

Deciding to start by looking into those disappearances, she packed everything back into the camper and started to drive.

She was in Hay-on-Wye by mid-afternoon, though driving the steep and lonely winding roads did not make the journey as easy as it should have been. Twice she found herself turning left on Watery Lane before realising she'd driven in a full circle. Eventually, she pulled the camper into a wide, sloping car park on Oxford Road, half in the shadow of a low, squat library building. She climbed out and looked up; painted in a yellowish shade of magnolia, the library was a neat, long building sheltered by a jutting square rooftop.

She went in and found the computer bank, noting

that the few cars she'd seen in the parking lot – which she assumed must serve for most of the town's visitors rather than just the library – and the couple of patrons milling about in here were the first people she'd seen in a little while. Not counting Lewis, Adrian or the men in black, of course.

'All right,' she said, logging on with a library account that she hadn't used in over a year. She had always been good at remembering numbers, for whatever reason; that was just about the only thing her father had ever complimented her on, when he was still kicking around. Perhaps she'd leaned into it as a result. Whatever the case, she was glad that it had served her now.

Ignoring the temptation to check in on her mother, Rachel opened up the library archives and started to drift through newspaper articles. Gritty scans flickered past her as she browsed front pages and headlines. The old man hadn't mentioned anyone by name, nor any more details, so she had little hope of utilising the search function.

Still, she tried, searching first for "disappear".

*Is local fruit and veg trade **disappear**ing? We look into…*

*…menace Wye fishermen finally **disappear** after police involvement…*

*…third hiker **disappears** in Black Mountains.*

That was the one. She clicked, briefly read through the article. Three disappearances in two years, each about seven or eight months from the last. There were photographs of all three: three women, two of them photographed in hiking gear. Three smiling faces.

Three women.

She kept digging, scanning articles from the same paper between six and nine months of the last disappearance. In one of the later editions, she found mention of a fourth hiker. Another woman, also photographed. Smiling as though she hadn't a care in the world.

Using the search function again, she found a headline that screamed ***Black Mountains*** *claim two more victims as recent spate of **disappearances** continues.*

And another photograph, this time of a young couple. Gritty pixels showed her the grinning face of a woman in her mid-twenties, blonde hair pressed back in a ponytail, blue waterproof clinging to her with a heavy looking rucksack on her back. Her partner, a black woman with a blood-red coat, seemed to be the one who had taken the photograph; her arm was extended toward the reader, her hand out of the frame. Behind them, the Black Mountains were sprayed with ripe, yellow gorse.

And a shape…

Rachel blinked, scrolling to zoom in on the image. The shape was blurry, almost undiscernible, but there was definitely something… a smudge of black, a smear of something moving through the gorse. And a flash of silver at its neck, a tiny pinprick of white and grey where the sunlight caught on something metal.

A creature. A beast. *The* Beast.

She swallowed, kept looking. Searched for "beast" and had one article return:

*Black Mountain **Beast** slaughters five in six months.*

She blinked. Checked the date of the article. Christ, this was only last year… the creature was getting hungrier. She read on:

*…June marks yet another victim for the so-called "**Beast**" that has frightened locals and steered away visitors for the last 25 years. This morning, police found the remains of a young woman, identity as yet unknown, who had been complete exsanguinated. Drained of blood, the body was damaged irreparably by what could only be the creature that, seemingly, has made its lair in the Mountains and now*

'Christ almighty,' Rachel murmured, scrolling down to look for a photograph. She found one, of the site whereby the body had been found – though the photographer had waited, presumably out of respect, for the body itself to be removed – and saw flecks of blood scattered in the dirt. And prints – the thick, knotted pawprints of a large dog.

And boot-prints, too. Faded, scuffed as though something had half-heartedly attempted to scraped them away.

Something, or *someone*.

Frowning, Rachel scrolled back up to check something. Female. The victim had been another woman.

A few was a trend, but every single one? That was a pattern. And creatures don't discriminate, she thought.

But monsters do.

'Memory card,' she said quietly, patting her pockets. Nothing. It was gone. In the camper? She tried to remember if she'd changed her jeans when she'd reached the layby. Or perhaps it had fallen out of her pocket…

In the corner of the computer screen, a small window popped up with a message telling her that her sixty minutes were almost up. She swore, glancing about, and continued scrolling, making sure she'd gotten everything she could from the article. When she reached the next page, she stopped.

Froze. Read it again.

Casper Hyde, 83, dies of lung cancer.

'Adrian's dad,' she whispered. She scrolled up again, looking once more at the photograph of the prints in the dirt. The wellington prints that were only half-covered, as though whoever had left them had his mind on other things. 'Oh, Adrian, no…'

Adrian Hyde had drained half a bottle of Jameson's when, for the second time that day, someone broke him out of half-dazed reverie with a knock on the door.

He scowled into the glass in his hand, swilling sticky, sweet fluid and wincing as the small reflection in the whiskey distorted and warped, ruining his face. 'Fuck off, Lewis,' he murmured, 'you've said your piece, you old bastard. Now leave me *alone.*'

The knocking persisted. And he knew that it wasn't Lewis, for the rap of knuckles on wood was too strong, too solid. He knew the old man's bony knocking too well. Well, whoever it was, they'd only heard about the tragedy and come to wish him well. News travelled fast, in a place like this. Well, they could sod off with their well wishes and leave him to his own, couldn't they?

knok knok knok

'Oh, for fuck's sake,' he grunted. Tipping the rest of the glass down his throat, he sat up from the kitchen table and peered up through the window above the washbasin. Two dark shapes on the porch, though he couldn't make out much more than that. One was speaking to the other quietly.

Unease settling in his stomach, Adrian returned to the kitchen, unscrewed the cap of the whiskey bottle, and drank deeply.

The men outside knocked again.

'All right,' he said, 'what do you want?'

Cautiously, he headed for the front door. Looking out through the pebbled glass, he recognised the two men as two of the black-suits he'd seen at the site of the collision. The man with the grey hair and his bald, dark-skinned partner.

Adrian opened the door and smiled warmly out at them. 'Hello, fellas,' he said.

Silence. For a moment they just looked at him. The grey-haired man had removed his sunglasses and Adrian saw that his eyebrows were just a shade whiter than the thinning hair of his scalp. The same white brushed the man's temples in thick streaks; he was not old, but stress had weathered his face. Behind him, the second man stood with his hands on his hips, black blazer tugged back a little from his chest.

There was a leather holster wound around his shoulder, and Adrian saw the hilt of a great big pistol stuffed into his armpit. A great big windsucker of a thing.

He swallowed. 'What can I do for you?'

The grey man looked him up and down. 'Mr. Hyde?'

Adrian nodded.

'Come with us.'

'What?' he frowned.

'Come with us,' the grey man repeated, his voice thick and gravelly.

'Why? Who are you?' He looked from one to the other. Remembered that there had been a third, at the collision site. The tall man in the waistcoat. 'Where's your buddy?'

'Who we are is of no concern to you,' the Black man said. He had a thin, pale scar dashing through his right eyebrow, Adrian noticed. 'We have reason to believe you know what attacked the lorry earlier today. That is all.'

'And – what – you're taking me for questioning?'

The grey man smiled thinly. 'Something like that,' he said, and he reached into his jacket.

Adrian reacted on instinct. His arm jerked forward and he swung the door shut, slamming it into the frame. He reached up to slide the bolt across – and recoiled as a shadow crashed into the pebbled glass and the window shattered, spraying him with sharp-edged shards. He cried out and staggered back as the butt of the pistol withdrew from the ragged frame.

'What the hell?!' Adrian yelled.

The doorhandle twisted.

His eyes widened and he leapt forward, pressing himself to the wall and fumbling above the broken window for the bolt. He jammed it across with a *click*—

And saw the barrel of the windsucker pointed at his eyeball through the shattered hole in the door.

Adrian ducked. There was a *crack!* and a chunk of plaster was ripped from the wall behind his head. He scrambled away from the door, wailing as something smashed into it outside – a boot, or a knee – Christ, they were kicking it down—

The door crashed open and Adrian threw his hands above his head.

The grey man stepped inside, glass crunching beneath polished, black boots. He looked at Adrian, then nodded back in Scarface's direction. Both men holstered their dirty great pistols.

'What the fuck are you doing?' Adrian hissed. 'Who the fuck are you? You're not police, and you're not—'

Scarface stepped forward, blotting out the light from outside. He was a big man, bigger than his partner, and his face was a stoic mass of gritted teeth. 'Doesn't matter who we are,' he echoed. 'Only matters that we have a job to do.'

'Where do you keep it?' the grey man said.

Adrian backed up against the wall, keeping his hands high above his head. 'I don't know what you're talking about,' he said. 'But I won't stand for this. You can't just come in here and break down my door and—'

'Where's the fucking creature?' Scarface said, and then the gun was in his hand again and pointed at Adrian's throat.

Adrian frowned. 'The… the thing that attacked my sheep?'

'Don't play stupid,' the grey man said. 'That won't end well for you.'

'I don't know what you—'

'You know where the creature is,' said Scarface. 'You're keeping it somewhere. Hiding it.'

Adrian shook his head. 'I don't… why would I…

Jesus, what, do you think I'm in cahoots with this creature? That I let it kill my livestock? Christ, what do you think I am?!'

The grey man shrugged. 'Insurance fraudster. Sick psychopath. Vampire-loving sonofagun. I don't know, and we don't care. Show us where you keep it.'

'Show us what's in the barn,' Scarface murmured.

Adrian turned to him. Cocked an eyebrow. 'What?'

'We saw a barn on the way in,' Scarface said. 'Seems a good place to start looking for your little... pet.'

'No,' Adrian said.

'No?' the grey man said, stepping up close.

'No,' Adrian said. 'You need a warrant. I'm not—'

'I can assure you we don't,' said the grey man. His breath smelled like peppermint.

'Show us the barn,' Scarface said.

'*No.*'

Scarface stepped forward, poking the very tip of the pistol into the flesh of Adrian's throat. 'Show. Us. The barn.'

'Shoot him,' said the grey man suddenly. 'I'll find the keys.'

'What, no – no, don't shoot,' Adrian pleaded.

Scarface thumbed down the hammer with a deafening *click*. 'Please, no – okay! I'll show you the barn. Okay. But you won't like what's in there.'

The grey man smiled that thin smile again. 'Sounds promising,' he said.

Cool, blue late-afternoon light washed across the top of the T1 camper, draping it in the dusky shadows that filtered through the low gorse and scuffed hedges of the foot of the mountain.

Rachel moved quickly, stealing up the hillside in the fading light. She snapped off branches and thorny growths of wood as she hiked up, piling them into a rucksack already stuffed with kindling and firelighters.

When she reached the spot where she felt she'd seen the TrailCam, she spent a good half-hour searching for it. Finding it in a clump of bushes, she stalked behind it and moved to the lockbox. The padlock lay smashed on the ground. Bending down to open the box, she grabbed the hand axe and buried the blade into the earth beside her with a satisfying *shck* sound. She took the length of rope and fastened it into a haphazard noose, winding the loop around her arm and testing its tightness.

'That'll do,' she murmured, exploring the

surrounding shrubs until she found a clear spot. Crouching, she gently built a small fire in the earth and lit it, recoiling from a surprising *whoomph* of warmth.

And she waited.

Time slipped by slowly, and eventually she sat on her rump in the dirt, looking out into the fields and rolling roads of the surrounding countryside. The mountain was quiet, the only sound the soft crackling of flames. But something would come. Something had to…

She flexed her fingers around the handle of the axe and gripped it tight, tilting the blade back and forth and watching the firelight glint off its sharp, steel face.

'Come on…' she whispered.

The other side of the little knot of shrubs she'd hidden behind, she heard a crunch. The sound of a heavy paw on broken wood. She froze.

Moments later, another.

Gingerly laying more wood on the fire, reluctant to make any sound, Rachel peered through the shimmering heat haze into the approaching dusk and saw a shape moving through the earth.

***

Adrian led the men in black to the barn around the back of the farmhouse, trembling a little as they moved through the fading afternoon light. Their shadows fell long and silent across him, drowning any hopes of dashing away and leaving them to see for themselves.

In the doorway of the barn he stopped, keys in hand. The low, red-painted building was splashed with patches of mottled grey disrepair, its white frame now a pasty brown. The colour of earth. Dry paint peeled and cracked. Through gaps between the slatted boards, pebbled evening light filtered through the husk of the barn, sprayed in through holes and cracks the other side of the building. 'I can promise you,' he said slowly, 'you're not going to like what's in here.'

'Just open the door, farm boy,' Scarface said, reaching again for the gun in his jacket.

Adrian drew in a deep breath, nodded, and turned back to the door. Bracing himself, he slid the key into the lock and turned it with a *click*.

The door swung open, and he gestured inside.

Dark shadows filled the interior of the barn. Both the black-suited men pulled out their pistols as they stepped over the threshold. 'In you go, fellas,' Adrian said, slipping the keys back into his pocket. 'Like what you see?"

Scarface stepped into the shadows, cautiously swinging his pistol into each corner.

The grey man turned. 'There's nothing in here,' he said. 'The hell is this?'

'I told you you wouldn't like what was in here,' Adrian shrugged. 'You come here looking for some creature… you won't find it in my barn. Or on my farm at all, for that matter. You ought to be looking up in the hills.'

'Don't tell me where we ought to be looking,' the grey man scowled. Behind him, Scarface tramped softly through scattered earth and hay. The empty barn waited patiently, silently.

'If it's not here,' Scarface said, 'where is it?'

'Like I said, I don't know. But…' Adrian swallowed. 'I know who might.'

Rachel gripped the axe tight and slowly, tentatively, stood up. In the light of the small fire she'd made, she saw the prickles and thorns of the mountainside shrubs and the thick knots of gorse all around her. Moonlight began to peel through the dusk and the mountain was bathed in a soft, flickering amber.

The creature was gone. She was positive she'd heard it – heard *something* – but looking about now, she could see no sign of anything at all. Just her own timid shadow, twisting and writhing in the firelight.

Wood popped and wheezed on the campfire as she stepped forward, brandishing the axe and moving slowly out from behind the shrubs. Her footfalls were soft and near-silent on the dusty earth. Above her, ribbons of blue moonlight cascaded down the mountain. Below, the landscape was growing dark.

She turned to look back – and saw the creature watching her in the firelight.

'Oh, Jesus,' she whispered. Its face glowed bright and dangerous, eyes lit ablaze by the flames. It slavered hungrily in the dark, its teeth connected by strings of gluey saliva. Ichor stained its gums, the black, dried blood of all those poor animals it had drained.

It stepped forward – and she saw a flicker of silver at its neck. Lit by the firelight, a steel collar glinted in the dark. There was a *crack!* and the creature recoiled, withdrawing into the shadows around the small campfire.

Rachel looked up. 'You,' she said.

Gwynne Lewis stood behind the creature, a small, black remote in his hand. He jabbed a button on the slim device and the collar around the creature's neck crackled with electricity. The beast whimpered.

'I told you to leave,' Lewis said solemnly. Beside

him, the creature growled softly, its snarls a soft hum that resonated across the crackling fire. 'But you wouldn't listen.'

Chapter Nine
PUP

1995

Gwynne Lewis slogged through the mist, letting it roll around his ankles as he tramped quietly across the field. Around him, the moans and brittle cries of the goats filled the air; the morning light was dull and sombre, and their pitiful, almost mournful sounds turned the pallid squall of the morning into a pall of funeral grey.

Still, he loved being out here. He would tend to the sheep next – it was almost time to shear, and he planned to inspect their plump hides as he filled up the feeding troughs and get some idea of just when they might need rounding up. More work. It was always more work. But that was all right. Since Maureen… no, he'd promised himself that he wouldn't talk about her. Wouldn't think about her, not after what had happened.

Keep busy, he thought, moving through the mist to the trough. Around him, a small herd of alpine goats bustled and bumped at his thighs with their stubby horns, bleating softly for their food.

'All right, all right...' he murmured, finally opening the lid of the plastic bucket in his arms. Silence fell around him, almost instant, and he smiled thinly. 'Oh, I see how it is,' he said as he started to tip the bucket out into their trough. 'You're not here for *me...*'

Grains scattered in the trough and it began to fill. He stepped back, the bucket swinging in his hand as he turned.

'Come on then,' Lewis said, 'what are you waiting...'

They were gone.

'...for?'

He blinked, peering into the early morning fog and searching for any sign of movement. But no, the tiny herd that had followed him across here had disappeared. He heard a distant, muted bleating carry on the mist; they were over in the far corner of the field. His heart fell back out of his mouth and into its rightful position in his chest. Christ, for a moment he thought something had happened to them. No, they had simply… what? Gotten distracted? Scared away?

Was there something over there?

As he crossed the field in the direction of the muffled wails, Lewis thought that something about the sound was off, was wrong… they sounded distressed, strangled, like they were scared of something.

As he neared, he saw their silhouettes bulge and blossom in the fog, huddled in a tight knot of grey and brown in the very corner of the field. Heads bowed, horns pressed almost into the earth. There was something down there, in the middle of the huddle, something wriggling…

'Hey,' Lewis called. 'What's going on here, loves?'

The bleating continued, louder now and more frantic, more strained with concern and wry emotion.

'Hey!' he yelled, clapping his hands together, and the silhouetted shapes dispersed, spreading out into the field around him.

If Maureen were here, she'd have told him to leave it alone. Grabbed his hand and dragged him away and out of the field. She'd have known something wasn't right – and he did, too, but he couldn't just leave it there, not all on its own…

'Good god,' he said, 'what are you?'

He knelt in the grass where the goats had been huddled only moments before and stared in awe at the thing they'd gathered around.

It lay in the clipped grass, its body slick with a mixture of early morning dew and a strange, greyish kind of mucus. Its chest was deflated and sunk between ribs that poked sharply against the leathery skin, and it heaved with each ragged breath.

'Christ,' Lewis whispered, looking around him. All the goats had gone, disappeared back into the mist.

The thing looked harmless, hardly the size of a small terrier – perhaps the size of a cat, he thought, or a deflated rugby ball with bony legs. It was canine in build, that was sure, and looked almost like the pup of some hybrid thing bred for hunting; its jaws certainly looked bulky and strong enough for that.

But it wasn't a dog. Its skin, for one thing. The creature was entirely hairless, and its hide was almost reptilian, though the scales were smooth and grey. Like sharkskin, perhaps. Tiny quivers on its back, like the spines of a hedgehog only scattered sparsely and inky black, trembled as it breathed, a long, wiry tail tucked into its hind legs. Its claws were sharp, big paws indicating the kind of size it might reach as it matured.

But it was only a baby. And it was wounded, he

saw, its rump and flank torn so violently that he could see strips of muscle beneath.

The creature's eyes opened. Thin lids peeled apart and it mewled softly as bright, yellow slits widened between them.

'Oh, you poor baby,' Lewis said quietly, bending down to slip his hands beneath the creature. Gently, he scooped it into his arms, ignoring its quiet whimpering. 'Come on, sweetie, let's go get you fixed up.'

Standing slowly, blood oozing from the creature's slippery form and seeping into his clothes, Gwynne Lewis looked up toward the empty barn across the farm, a smudge of red and grey in the mist, and started to carry the creature over to it.

2021

Adrian peeled up the latch and pushed the wide, crooked gate open, looking around before stepping through it and beckoning the men in black through after him. Scarface and the grey man followed, thick, black muck clotting the polished laminate of their shoes. They were as out of place here as he would have been in the city; two men in crisp, black suits with earth spattering their calves. It didn't seem right. But then, none of this did.

Please let me be wrong, Adrian thought, leading the way silently across the farm. To his left and right, empty fields had become vast crop plots, and grain blew softly in the wind, gravelly heads rustling together as the breeze forced them to dance. God, he thought, please just let me be wrong…

Lewis's farm was quiet, a massive expanse of hollow ground with a crumbling wooden fortress in the middle of it all. He was away, he must have been. If he was here, he would have come out by now. Would have chased them away. Still, Adrian couldn't help but keep an eye on the front door of the old farmhouse as he led his co trespassers across his neighbour's land and toward that big, red barn.

The barn that had been locked for years, that he'd never thought about twice…

Oh, *Christ*, let me be wrong.

He turned as they walked and nodded curtly at the grey man. 'Where's the other guy?' he said. 'Back on the road, there were three of you. You two and the tall fella. Where's he gone, what's he doing?'

'None of your business,' Scarface said bluntly.

Adrian looked at the grey man's partner and cocked an eyebrow. 'Nothing good, then,' he said.

'Leave it alone, sunshine,' the grey man said. 'It's

not for you to know.'

Adrian shrugged, turning his head back to the barn and continuing along the scratched dirt path through the farmyard. The barn loomed above them, almost as big as the house and painted in long-faded shades of deep, blood red. White trim had peeled off rutting, rotting wooden beams and the doors that had once looked inviting were a grim, buck-toothed mouth of mottled slabs.

Padlocked. Twice.

Adrian swallowed, pulling back as the men in the black suits pressed toward the door. He watched as the older of the two pulled a slim, angular device that looked a little like a miniature crowbar from his jacket and jimmied it into the first lock. It split open and the bolt came loose. Behind him, Scarface pulled out his gun and braced it, resting the barrel on one wrist as he aimed carefully at the closed door. Ready for whatever might be on the other side.

'Ready?' the grey man asked, and Scarface nodded.

The second padlock cracked open, and the chains swung loose. Pulling his own gun, the older man brought his free hand up to the doorhandle and counted from three.

Adrian drew in a breath.

The doors screamed open and the men in black

swung through, plunging into the darkness of the barn. Adrian stood back a little, watching as their shapes disappeared in the shadows. 'Clear!' one of them yelled, from deep within the barn.

'Nothing here,' the other confirmed. Adrian let his breath go, relief flooding his chest. Oh, thank god he'd been wrong. It wasn't Lewis. Of course it wasn't. Lewis wouldn't—

'Wait, what's this?'

'*Ho*—ly shit…'

Oh, god.

Oh, *god*.

Adrian stepped through the doors and looked around. Dark shapes swum through the dirt, filtered shafts of light peeling in through cracks in the walls and spraying dust particles in the air with gold. Slowly, cautiously, the man reached behind him and pushed the doors wide open, letting sunlight flood into the barn.

'Oh, hell…'

The barn's dusty floor was covered with hay, a thick blanket of it shunted into piles and pillows at the edges of the space. The crusty yellow bed was smeared with blood, drops of it spattered in wild arcs and pooled into shallow, sticky puddles in which small chunks of meat swam and decayed. The stink of mould mingled with the scent of pennies on the air.

Bolted to a thick, wooden pillar in the middle of the room were three shackles, one of which was twice the size of the others. One for the neck, Adrian thought, and two for the thing's legs. Jesus Christ. Its lair had never been up in the Mountains; it had been here all along…

But where was it now? The shackles hung limp from their chains, dropped into the hay beneath. Rusted iron clamps had been unlocked and opened. Someone – *Lewis* – had let the thing loose.

'Look over here, man,' Scarface said, his voice coming from the end of the barn. The grey man walked cautiously across to him. Adrian looked in their direction.

A wide, metal food trough had been laid against the wall. It was old, rusted, sharp-edged. He recognised it as one that had disappeared from the goats' field weeks after they'd been butchered.

It killed your own livestock, Adrian thought, and you still kept it here? Fed it? Christ, you…

His train of thought drifted, abandoned him, as he looked up.

Hanging above the food trough were three bodies. The corpses swung from chains bolted to the ceiling, hooks plunged into bloated, fleshy shoulders and stomachs.

'Oh, fuck…'

Two hikers that he recognised from the newspaper, and a third woman that he didn't.

Drip.

A single bead of blood swelled at one woman's throat, oozed down her face, and dropped loudly into the food trough beneath the gently swinging cadavers. Mouths open, eyes wide and horrified – Christ, had they still been *alive* when Lewis had hung them?

Adrian balked. The woman on the left had been carved up, her legs and stomach slashed by an axe so that stripes of deep purple – dried, now, and crusted over and congealed – ruined her body. The one in the middle had had her throat slashed. Or broken open at least, so violently that her head was twisted back and he could see ribbons of slick cartilage through the wound.

And they had all bled out into the trough for Lewis's awful pet to feed upon.

'Where is he now?' Scarface said.

Adrian's eyes passed from corpse to corpse, his face turning white as nausea swept through him. Oh, Lewis, how could you…

'Hey,' Scarface said. Adrian lowered his eyes. 'I'm talking to you, shithead.'

Adrian blinked. 'What?'

'I said, where is he now?'

'Oh. I… I don't know. I last saw his car heading for the Mountains.'

'Is it possible he could have taken the creature with him?' the grey man said.

Adrian looked up, at the slowly dripping bodies hanging from the barn's ceiling. 'Doesn't look like he ever has before.'

No; in fact, it looked a whole lot like Lewis had been the one with the lair up in the Black Mountains. Like he had killed these women and dragged them back here for his Beast to live off. All the while, it had been right here…

'What do we do?' Scarface whispered. 'We have to get a live specimen,' the grey man said quietly. He glanced back at Adrian, then looked away again. 'The boss has been off on one since the American let us down—'

'The American died,' Scarface said. 'Remember?'

'Well, either way, we need to do better than he did.'

Adrian took a step back. Another.

'All right, well… should we wait here, for him to bring it back?'

'If he does, it's likely he'll be bringing another body back with him,' the grey man said.

'True. But what's one more?'

Quietly, Adrian stepped back through the doors, his eyes never leaving the backs of their bowed heads.

'What if he doesn't come back? He's seen us now, he knows we're onto him. What if he's taken the creature someplace to set it free?'

Adrian whistled.

They both turned at once, the grey man's eyes widening as he realised what was about to happen.

'Good luck,' he said, smiling thinly, and he slammed the doors shut.

Tightening the chains quickly as he heard scuffling footsteps bolting for the door, Adrian swore and fought with the ruined padlock. The locking cylinder had been shot out, but if he could just—

The lock jutted back into place with a *click* and he stepped back as the two men started to hammer on the doors, cursing and yelling.

Adrian staggered back, running a hand through his hair as the slamming on the door turned to a pounding.

'Shit,' he said, and he turned and looked toward Lewis's farmhouse. 'What have you done, old man?'

＊＊

The key to the farmhouse was hidden beneath a coarse welcome mat upon which was printed *Off My Land* along with a cartoonish farmer character brandishing a shotgun; at one point, Adrian had thought that was funny.

Fumbling with the lock, he stepped into the front hall and – out of habit – wiped his boots on the mat inside. He was sure Lewis had gone, but he had to check. Had to make sure the old man wasn't in here somewhere.

'Lewis?' he called, moving through the hallway like a burglar. He felt like one. 'Lewis, you old prick! You here?'

He turned through a low doorway and into the old man's kitchen.

On a round, wooden table in the middle of the room, he saw an empty tumbler, a near-empty bottle of Jameson's, and a photo album, spread open. The old man was drunk. That much was clear. But where—

Adrian saw the note and stepped over to the table, picking it up to read it. Lewis's handwriting was scrawled and messy, not the crisp, cursive script Adrian was used to.

I told you not to get those sheep, it said. And, in an even messier pen, *Whatever you find, don't trust the men in suits. They don't want the best for her.*

I do.

Adrian stuffed the note into his pocket and glanced down at the photo album on the table. It was open to the first page, and a smiling, younger Gwynne Lewis stood with an arm around the shoulders of another man.

Adrian's father.

Adrian shook his head, turning the page. A gritty, black-and-white image of the farm, taken from above, the fields filled with smudges of white. Back before it had all gone to shit; before the Beast…

He turned the page again, and he froze.

In the third photograph, Lewis knelt on the floor of the barn, a puppy cradled in his arms. He must have set the camera on a timer, for there was a blur of grey in the bottom where he'd rested it on a pillar at the edge of the barn.

No, the thing in his arms wasn't a puppy. Not really. Not at all.

It was the size of a cocker spaniel, and its hide was covered in scales. Thick, black spines lined its back, and a wiry tail was coiled around Lewis's arm. The pup – for it was surely a pup, even if it wasn't a dog – looked up at the old man with wide, round eyes, smiling with a sharp-toothed snout.

They looked good together. Master and hound, father and pup.

And in the next photograph, it had grown.

Adrian turned the pages silently, watching as the creature in the photos turned from a pup to a juvenile, from a juvenile to a mature animal. In one image, it stood at Lewis's knee, the old man bending down to scratch behind its pointed ears. In the next, it was the height of his hip and he didn't have to bend at all.

In the last, the creature was the size of a Great Dane, head bowed, teeth protruding from a snout that could no longer hold them. Its tail swept behind it, a thick, black noose with a pointed tip, and the dark, pointed quivers along its back were a foot long each. Its grey, reptilian skin was mottled and bumpy, its claws thick and cloven.

It was a monster.

Adrian slammed the book shut and went back into the hall, aware of the heavy smashing sounds coming from the barn. That door wouldn't hold them long, and one of them was still out there…

Stepping outside, he looked up, toward the Mountains, and saw a tiny spark of amber up in the dark.

Chapter Ten
RABID

The reptilian hound growled softly, its slavering teeth flashing in the firelight.

'I don't understand,' Rachel whispered, looking from the animal to the man standing beside it. Lewis looked back, his eyes black points. 'Why?'

The creature moved suddenly, lunging forward, firelight streaking its back as it smashed its teeth together and leapt at her—

There was a soft *crack!* and the creature's throat jerked. Just feet from her, it recoiled, shrinking back into itself. Hungry eyes desperately pawing at her body, the monster gritted its teeth as though something was physically pulling it back, keeping it anchored to the ground.

Heart in her mouth, Rachel saw that there was a collar around the thing's neck, a thick band of silver that fizzed with electricity. Tight enough that it strained the bunched muscles beneath, every few seconds she heard the distinct, muted tak of power passing through the wires.

Lewis stepped up and laid a hand carefully on the creature's head, stroking it softly between the ears.

'Get away from it,' Rachel said weakly, gripping the axe tight in her hand. Behind her, the rope lay forgotten on the floor, a loose knot snaking through the dry grass and earth. 'How do you know it won't—'

'Hurt me?' Lewis smirked. 'Oh, she would never.'

'It wouldn't? Then why the shock collar?' she asked, swallowing hard as her eyes flitted from man to beast, from coward to hound.

'If not for the collar, love, she would have ravaged you in seconds. Picked the flesh right off your body – cleanly, surgically… till you were nothing. The collar teaches her to exercise restraint.'

'There's a difference between teaching restraint and restraining,' Rachel said quietly, taking a single step back. Lewis mirrored her movement, stepping forward, firelight creasing the lines of his old face. The creature moved with him. 'Why are you doing this?'

Lewis said nothing.

'And why have you been warning people away from the Mountains?' she frowned. 'I don't… I don't understand. If you're working with this… this thing… then… oh.'

It made sense. All at once, it hit her.

It was never a warning. It was a *dare*.

'People like you,' Lewis said thinly, 'explorers, adventurers… you go digging where you're not wanted, warned against it or not. In fact, people like you tend to go exactly where you're warned not to. You see?'

'I do.'

'We've shared so many years,' Lewis said, smiling down at the creature. There was another *crack!* and it mewled softly, pushing the top of its skull into his curved palm. Asking to be pet. 'Twenty-six years ago, I lost my daughter. My Maureen. Cancer.'

'I'm sorry,' Rachel said, 'but—'

'Cancer. At fifteen. My wife left when the treatments became too much for our little girl, and I stayed right till the end. That's what I do, you see? I do what needs to be done.'

'I don't—'

'And then, the very same year my poor little girl was taken from me, something else was dropped into my lap.'

'You raised it,' Rachel whispered. 'Like a pet.'

'Not a pet. And not an *it*. She's part of the family,' Lewis snarled. 'A part of me. Do you know what they would've done to her, if I hadn't kept her alive? Kept her fed? The things I've done… the things I've sacrificed, just to feed her…'

'You killed people,' Rachel said. She looked at the axe in her hands. 'The lockbox, the camera… they're yours. What do you do, "warn" people up here and then follow them? Tie them up, cut them up and drag them back to the farm?'

'Better that they go missing up here than down in the village,' Lewis said quietly. 'I don't enjoy it, Rachel. But it's necessary. And if I didn't… *limit* her intake…'

Again, Rachel looked at the creature. It was the size of a small horse, and built like a Rottweiler. Its skull was profoundly canine, its jaws packed with sabre-teeth, its eyes a furious, glowing yellow. But it was hairless, its hide covered in thick, grey scales, and now that it was clearly lit by the campfire, she could see that it looked sick. Its neck and legs were scratched raw, blisters and boils coursing across its shoulders. It looked… mangy.

The spines along its back – thick, pointed quills jutting from its body and dripping with black ichor – trembled excitedly, shivering with every breath. A long, snake-like tail curled into a spike behind it.

'You should get away from it,' Rachel whispered. 'Look at it, Gwynne. That thing's not meant to be anyone's pet.'

Lewis's mouth twitched. 'Didn't you hear me?'

'All right, it's not meant to be *kept*. Is that better? Part of your family or not, if you let that thing go—'

Lewis smiled. He raised his hand, and Rachel finally saw the slender remote control he gripped in his palm. 'Enough,' he said. 'I'm bored.'

He pushed a button on the remote with a *click* and a jolt of electricity surged through the creature's collar.

'Kill,' he whispered, and the creature lunged.

Rachel staggered back as the creature burst toward her, raising the axe high and preparing to swing—

Teeth snapped in her face and the creature's head whipped to one side as another shock crashed through its body. Somewhere in the dark, Gwynne Lewis laughed as Rachel whimpered, the axe trembling in her grip.

'You're hurting it!' she yelled. The creature came back around and she heard a gentle buzzing, a dull throb coming from the collar around its neck as the thing lowered its head, haunches raised, and crept forward.

Long, glimmering strings of drool swung from its jaws as its yellow eyes narrowed.

'Call it off,' she said, looking into those eyes as they bristled with fire. 'Please, Gwynne, call it off and we'll talk.'

The creature took another step. Taunting her, its powerful legs pressed into the ground as it prepared to pounce. It moved like a panther, head low to the ground like a wolf's head, snout quivering with bloodlust.

'Call it off!'

The buzzing increased as the creature took another step. Closer, so close that she could smell the mange that was eating away at its body.

'Gwynne, please, stop this!'

'No,' he whispered, and the buzzing increased again.

The creature leapt suddenly, a roar exploding from deep within its belly as it pounced, teeth snapping in the air as its claws swiped at her face—

'Fuck!' Rachel yelled, and she swung the axe blindly into the dark.

***

Adrian Hyde pulled the A-Class up to the foot of the mountain and shut off the engine, basking for a moment in the dark silence that followed.

Drawing in a deep breath, he shoved the door open and stepped out of the Merc. Glancing up at the mountain, he saw rivers of shadow falling across the slope, and a small point of flickering amber halfway up. Shapes darted across the firelight. Christ, was he too late already?

Slamming the door shut, Adrian pulled his jacket tight and looked quickly around. Beside him, Rachel's T1 camper was parked haphazardly in the gravel at the edge of the road.

And behind it, a matte-black SUV with tinted windows.

'Shit,' Adrian murmured, gritting his teeth as he started up the hill.

There was a dry *crunch* and a knot of sparks flew into the dark as the axe blade smashed into the creature's collar. A soft twang as something broke, and then the dog froze.

Inches from her face, the creature drooled, breathing heavily, staring into her eyes. The shattered collar around its neck sparked again and she staggered back as it sloughed it off, its whole body twitching as it realised that the electricity coursing through it had stopped.

And then it turned to look back through the firelight at the man with the remote control.

Lewis pressed a button with a soft *click*. Pressed it again. Rachel heard him curse as he tried again, pawing at the remote. The creature moved slowly, stalking across the fire, leaving her behind as she panted, the axe trembling in her hand…

'Run,' she called across the fire, 'for god's sake, Gwynne, run—'

Lewis smiled. He tossed the remote into the fire, spreading his hands. Looking deep into the creature's eyes, his expression softened. No longer fearful but welcoming. 'She'd never hurt me,' he whispered. 'Collar or not, we're *family*, and she'd never—'

The beast pounced.

Rachel clamped a hand over her mouth to stifle a scream as the creature leapt onto its owner's throat, slamming him into the ground. It was a blur of grey and amber, a demon with flattened spikes along its back. Lewis shrieked as it plunged its snout into his chest and wrenched its head from side to side, tugging out ribbons of flesh and snapping them loudly as thick, wet clumps of meat popped between its teeth.

'No!' Lewis screamed, but it was too late. Blood erupted from his chest and the creature smashed its paws into his face, caving in his jaw with a heavy crunch and ripping his mandible apart. Rachel stumbled back as it dipped its mouth into Lewis's open neck and began to drink – and her ankle caught on the lockbox half-buried in the ground behind her.

The creature turned, head snapping around. The sick yellow of its eyes burned brightly as ropes of blood were flung from its jaws. Lewis's body twitched and convulsed violently beneath it as it kicked him away.

'No,' Rachel whispered, 'good doggy…'

Still chewing chunks of Lewis's throat, the creature turned and padded slowly back in her direction.

'Hey! Muttley!'

Rachel yelped as the dog knocked her onto her back, scrambling in the dirt. The creature turned at the sound of the newcomer's voice and Rachel looked up and past the abomination to see Adrian, his thin face bathed in the amber glow of the fire.

'Hey!' he yelled again. He whistled sharply, the sound echoing. 'Come here, you fucker!'

'No!' Rachel screamed. 'Adrian, it'll—'

Too late. Already the dog-thing was on its haunches, leaping across the fire toward the newcomer.

'No!' Rachel yelled again, scrabbling in the dirt for the rope she'd left tangled there. She found an end and curled her fingers around it, coughing up dirt. Standing shakily, she swung the noose above her head, flung it—

The coiled end of the rope smacked the creature's rump and snapped away, bouncing off its hide.

'Shit,' she yelled as the mad beast careened across the campfire, hardly noticing the flames as they surged across its body and fell away. It bounded over Lewis's still, sloppy mess of a cadaver and leapt—

Rachel yanked back the rope and flung it again.

The noose snapped around the dog's hind leg and she tugged it quickly, snagging the beast with a yelp. Its paw jerked back violently and something cracked as she held on, lengths of rope slipping through her hands and burning her palms with a slick, grinding wheeze.

Across the fire from her, Adrian bent to pick up the axe that had fallen in the dirt, came forward, raised it high—

'No!' she yelled again. 'Don't kill it!'

'What?!' he screamed. On the end of the rope, the dog-thing struggled, batting and clawing at it. It was still trying to get to Adrian, but once it realised that the length of rope connecting it to Rachel was really very short it would turn back and sever that connection – along with her arm – she was sure of it.

'If we can get it tied up, we can keep it here until… I don't know, until we can find somewhere out in the wild to release it! Somewhere it won't hurt anyone!'

'Are you nuts?'

Rachel tugged on the leash as the dog snapped at Adrian's heels. 'We don't have to kill it!' she yelled. 'It was only doing what it knows to do – it's just an animal, for Christ's sake!'

'It's a monster,' Adrian growled, and he raised the axe high above his head.

Then there was an explosion, a sick, black thunder crack and the smell of gunpowder, and hot white pain screamed up Rachel's leg as something smashed into her calf.

Rachel fell, shrieking as agony spread through her leg. The rope flew from her hands and the creature sprawled, momentarily dizzying itself in the firelight. She grabbed at her calf and her hands came away hot and sticky, a slick, wet warmth seeping over her ankle. The flesh beneath the fabric of her jeans was mashed to pulp; the bullet had passed right through bone and out the other side, leaving an entry wound in her shin the size of a tea saucer.

'Jesus!' she yelled, looking up to see what had shot her. She didn't get the chance. Another gunshot echoed, right in her ear – the sound of thunder, of an explosion of fireworks – and she screamed as

Adrian's face exploded in a cloud of red mist. The back of his skull opened and the look of surprise on his face was momentary, then it was gone. His teeth caved in, his head erupting.

He stood there for a moment, a great, sunken red hole in his mouth splitting with blood, and then slowly, unsteadily, he crumpled to his knees and fell onto his front in the dirt.

Adrian was dead.

'What the fuck?!' Rachel screamed. 'Jesus shitting Christ, what the—'

She went silent as a shadow fell across the firelight.

The man was tall, taller than he had seemed earlier, and dressed in a crisp, black suit. His skin was pale, even in the firelight, and the gun in his hand was a huge, dirty great bastard of a pistol.

The dog-thing scrambled in the earth, its legs tangled in the rope.

He headed toward it, his shadow dampening the flames. 'There's a good little bitch,' whispered the man in black.

'Don't kill it,' Rachel whispered. She could feel herself fading, black spots dancing at the edges of her vision as the pain in her leg spread up her whole body. She could feel the life running out of her. 'Please.'

'Oh, I wouldn't dream of it,' he said, and his voice was like honey. 'We've got plans for her. And for everything else out there…'

Rachel watched through a slurry of red fog as the man bent down, pulling something long and sharp from his black jacket and injecting it into the writhing creature's flank.

The animal went still.

And as the man in black bundled the Beast of the Black Mountains into his arms and stood, its tail draping into the shadows around him, Rachel faded out of consciousness and the world went totally, completely dark.

<u>Chapter Twelve</u>
THE DUST

When Rachel woke up, it was morning. Somewhere distant a cock was screaming; she imagined that was likely what had woken her.

She sat up stiffly, her ruined leg complaining violently. Her face was smeared with drool and grass. There was a little blood on her neck, caked there and cracking open. She massaged her throat and pulled away her hand to inspect it: not her own blood, at least. More concerning was the massive pool of crimson that had been pumped out of her calf. She felt light-headed and hungry – thirsty, more urgently. Grimacing, she bent forward and rolled up her trouser-leg to inspect the wound.

It had been patched up.

'What?' she murmured, lightly pawing at the bandages wound around her leg. The blood in the grass was mostly dry, congealed into a dark jelly, and the leg itself had been cleaned; she could no longer see the clean black pit of the bullet's entry or the savage rend in her flesh where it had punched out through the bone – it was all wrapped up in a compress, and quite expertly too.

There was no chance she'd be able to stand, she realised as a bolt of pain surged up her thigh. Gripping her leg tight as she clenched her teeth, she started to pat her pockets for her mobile, hoping she could at least call the air ambulance – or the local pub, otherwise, just someone who could get her out of here – but she froze when she saw what had happened around her.

The bodies were gone.

Taken away, presumably by the same person – or people – that had sorted out her calf. The man in black? The last she had seen of him, he'd been cradling the scaly dog-thing in his arms, preparing to take it away. Had he come back to take the corpses, too?

Where Adrian Hyde had lay in the grass, his head open and spilling tiny chunks of bone into the earth, there was no sign he'd ever been there save for a few spots of blood. Lewis's savaged body had been removed too, and though there was a little more blood where he had been, Rachel could already taste an oncoming rainstorm on the air; looking up, her suspicions were confirmed. The sky was grey and thick. Soon, the blood would be washed away, and there would be no trace of what had happened up here.

Maybe that wasn't so bad.

She was out of the hospital a week later – though, with express orders not to drive, she was forced to stay in the village a little longer. Her nights on the ward had been restless and disturbed, and her first night in the van was just as fitful. By the time morning came around again, she had exhausted herself to sleep, and she spent most of the day unconscious in the layby, her novel all but forgotten.

Poor Adrian…

In the evening, she gathered her crutches and limped to Gwynne Lewis's farm. She was unsurprised to see that the big red barn was empty; it smelled thickly of bleach and chlorine. The men in black had taken care of it.

Stepping outside the barn, she gazed up at the setting sun and fumbled in her jacket for her phone. Hesitantly, she dialled.

The woman on the other end of the line answered after three rings. 'Everything okay, love?'

Rachel closed her eyes, the warmth of the orange sky bathing her face. 'Hi, Mum. Just checking in. How are you doing?'

'Oh, love. We're okay. What's going on? You never call me.'

'Is Dad there?'

There was a pause on the other end. Then: 'No, love. He's not here right now.'

'Good. I just wanted you.'

'Sweetie? What's wrong?' her mother said.

'Nothing,' Rachel smiled. *I got shot in the leg. A man I didn't really know died saving my life. Oh, and did you know monsters exist?* 'Nothing, Mum. Just… wanted to hear your voice.'

'You should come over sometime.'

'I would,' Rachel sighed, 'Mum, you know I would, if it was only—'

'If it was only me,' the older woman said, her voice crackling a little. 'You know, your dad's a different man now, love. He's better.'

'Maybe,' Rachel said, leaning heavily on her crutch with a hiss of pain and looking toward the road. The fields around her were painted with the same soft pink as the banks of cloud smearing the sky. 'What else is new?'

'We've got a puppy,' her mother said.

Rachel froze.

'You should come meet him, at least. Lovely little boy. Croatian Shepherd. Gorgeous black fur. Like silk, he is.'

Rachel's mouth opened, but she didn't say anything.

'Rach?' her mother said. 'You there, sweetie? Everything okay?'

'He sounds great, Mum. I'll have to come see him, yeah.'

They spoke for a little longer, and when the sun had fully set and the sky was beginning to turn a deep, bruised purple, Rachel hung up the phone and turned to hobble back across the farm. She fancied a quick trip to the Lamplight Inn. The beer was pretty good round here, after all.

She passed the silhouette of a tractor as she moved slowly around the edge of the field, its shape enormous and lumbering. Titanic blades poked out of its mouth, blackened against the moonlight.

Something scuffled quietly beneath the tractor's undercarriage, claws raking the dirt as it sniffed.

Rachel paused, listening in the near-dark, her heart pounding with terror. A second passed. Nothing. She shook her head, chiding herself for getting so spooked. Nothing, she thought. Just a rat.

She left, and a pair of tiny, glowing yellow eyes drilled into her back from beneath the tractor. A moment later a second pair joined the first, and then a third blinked open in the dark.

The litter returned to their catch, a pregnant badger sprawled on its belly in the dark beneath the giant machine, and gorged the coppery fluid from its spine, rolling in the blood and batting greedily, playfully at each other with black, scaly paws.

Epilogue
FILM

The edges of the room were impossibly dark, but the centre was filled with a soft, pulsing blue light that flickered and darted as the images on the monitors changed. The screens were arranged in a tall, wide arc atop a horseshoe of plain black desks, a dozen of them on each side of a large central display. The man in the chair leant back as he watched, a mug with *World's Best Cryptid Hunter* printed on it gripped in one hand. He was humming along to the Isley Brothers tape playing on a small, flat speaker on the desk. Files were scattered before him among an array of keyboards and control panels.

He had removed his black tie, and it hung over the chair behind him. His collar was open.

'Anything interesting?' came a voice from behind him.

The man turned, cocking an eyebrow as he sipped from his mug. 'Didn't hear you come in,' he said, setting the mug down.

The tall, thin man who had entered the room kept his eyes on the monitors, ignoring the man in the chair. His eyes were white points in the eerie blue light; his face was thin. His black suit was punctuated by a dull blue waistcoat.

'Look at this,' the man in the chair said, turning back to the screens. He pressed a few tabs on the nearest keyboard and an image was transferred with a brief flash of static from one of the monitors to the main display. 'We pulled a memory card off one of the bodies. The old guy. Looks like it had a bunch of TrailCam footage on it.'

'And?'

'And,' the man in the chair said, hitting *Play*, 'looks like there were two of them out there. Not just the one.'

The thin man nodded. 'Dispatch an agent.'

'Already sent two out there,' the man in the chair said. 'Told them to look for a nest, too.'

'Good work. Keep it up, Rogers,' the thin man said, clapping the other lightly on the shoulder before turning to leave. 'And put that tie back on.'

Rogers grinned, listening for the soft close of the door before playing the footage again.

On the screen, a pair of shadowy shapes with long, whip-like tails padded across the hillside. He skipped forward. There was the old guy again, axe in hand. He had enough footage of this guy butchering hikers to put together a slasher movie.

He paused the film when the woman entered the frame for the first time.

Rachel, her name was. She had been left at the scene after the creature was impounded. He had been strongly against that decision.

He had a feeling that she was going to be trouble for the agency down the line.

<u>A NOTE FROM THE AUTHOR</u>

Thank you for reading *Red Sky All Night*. As an independent author every single person reading my work is so valued and I can't express how much your time means to me. For more of my books, follow me on Instagram @heath_horrorwriter or check out my website derekheathhorror.com where I'll keep you updated on future releases.

I hope you enjoyed! If so, please leave a review on Amazon if you can. I'd love to know what you thought.

www.ingramcontent.com/pod-product-compliance
Lightning Source LLC
Chambersburg PA
CBHW031250210726
48287CB00003B/978